DEVIL IN THE PITCH

A NOVEL

FAITH FRANKLIN

WHISTLE FIG PUBLISHING

Copyright © 2023 Faith Franklin

All rights reserved

The characters and events portrayed in this book are fictitious. Any similarity to real persons, living or dead, is coincidental and not intended by the author.

No part of this book may be reproduced, or stored in a retrieval system, or transmitted in any form or by any means, electronic, mechanical, photocopying, recording, or otherwise, without express written permission of the publisher.

ISBN-13: 979-8218242787

Cover design by: Karam Alani
Published by Whistle Fig Publishing
Printed in the United States of America

Thank you to my beautiful daughters and sister for reading—re-reading— and re-re-reading. Love you all!

Hello Darkness, My Old Friend

                                        PAUL SIMON

CONTENTS

Title Page
Copyright
Dedication
Epigraph
The Murder

Chapter One	1
Chapter Two	16
Chapter Three	28
Chapter Four	36
Chapter Five	44
Chapter Six	53
Chapter Seven	62
Chapter Eight	76
Chapter Nine	88
Chapter Ten	91
Chapter Eleven	105
Chapter Twelve	112
Chapter Thirteen	119
Chapter Fourteen	122
Chapter Fifteen	129

Chapter Sixteen	135
Chapter Seventeen	146
Chapter Eighteen	153
Chapter Nineteen	164
Chapter Twenty	170
Chapter Twenty-one	178
Chapter Twenty-two	195
Chapter Twenty-Three	204
Chapter Twenty-four	209
Chapter Twenty-five	216
Chapter Twenty-Six	225
Epilogue	229
	233
Food for Thought	234
About the Author	235

THE MURDER

Night of The Murder

9:49 p.m.

Several moments pass before Kimber realizes the intolerable shrieking she hears comes from her own mouth. She is desperate to stop the noise escaping her, but it's no use, and the wailing continues. She is left having to stifle the noise with her hands.

The socialite has found her husband dead at the foot of the grand staircase in their very comfortable Nashville home. His head is cocked at an unnatural angle. His eyes sprung wide open. The handle of a large knife protrudes from his chest. A shock of crimson weeps into the fibers of his white dress shirt.

Her guests, who were laughing and drinking only moments ago, gather behind her, their mouths agape. The women are clutching at their men to save them from the shocking scene; several of them hysterical.

Collin steps up and takes charge. Putting his hands on Kimber's shoulders, he turns her away from the body and embraces her. He wants to soak in the feeling of her body folded into his. But Kimber has traded her screams for deep, heaving sobs, shaking them both and jolting him back to the situation at hand.

"Okay," Collin starts, "somebody dial 911."

One of the soccer guys speaks up, "Already on it."

Collin hands Kimber over to his wife, Beth. "Alright." We should all go back to the living room and stay together. The police will want statements from all of us."

As the crowd leaves the foyer for the living room, Collin's eyes fall on Jake for the last time, and his mouth curls up in a smile. "Awe, buddy," he croons, "this is such a good look for you!" He turns to join the others before adding, under his breath, "Burn in hell, you son of a bitch. You deserved it."

CHAPTER ONE

Detective Sol Parker
The Carter Residence Crime Scene
Night of the Murder

It's almost 11:00 p.m. when I turn onto the tree-lined street—Cliff's Edge Lane. The call came as I slipped off my pants, ready to crawl into bed with my wife. That's typical. I don't mind too much, though. Sleep doesn't come easy to me. I'm afraid it's an unfortunate side effect of the job.

When dispatch gave me the address, I was intrigued. A homicide call out this way happens once in a blue moon. The last time I answered a call from this wealthy suburb was to investigate a murder-suicide. It was my first case as lead detective. I was thirty-four years old.

It was one of those—*if I can't have you, no one can*—scenarios. The husband, a successful psychiatrist, couldn't accept that his wife wanted to leave him for another man. So he made sure she never would, stabbing her eighty-eight times before taking his own life. I'm telling you, it was a hell of a scene to cut my teeth on.

FAITH FRANKLIN

As I approach the address given, a mass of chaos rolls out in front of me. I count at least six cruisers and two crime scene vans sitting on the road at skewed angles, lights on—half a dozen civilian cars flank both sides of the street. I drive my beater straight up the middle, sandwiching it in as far as it will go, which isn't far enough. It's uphill and still a fair distance away, sad news for me and my bum knee.

I rummage around in my glove box, trying to find my cache of pain pills, grabbing handfuls at a time: napkins, old receipts, oil change records, lip balm, nasal spray, etcetera. I spread everything out on the passenger seat.

Three handfuls in, the amber-colored bottle I'm searching for peeks out of the pile. The bottle has someone else's name on the label. But that person didn't need them anymore. Why let them go to waste when they can offer me a little relief?

I unscrew the lid and shake the contents into my hand—twelve pills left. *Shit*. I pop three in my mouth and send them down my throat with what's left of my energy drink. The bottle goes deep into my pocket.

While I debate whether I should give the pain pills time to kick in before attempting the hill, an all-too-familiar feeling comes over me. It's something I feel in my bones—a foreboding.

Unable to sit with the dread, I pull the handle and push out the door, allowing the damp air to rush in and take hold of me. After a short *you-can-do-this* pep talk, I unpack my body from the car and attempt to straighten myself out.

Head down, I lean into the hill, pressing forward—one step at a time.

It's been four years since a truck plowed into me while I

was waiting at a stoplight. The man behind the wheel was an eighty-two-year-old Army vet who suffered a massive heart attack on the way home from the grocery store. When the fire department extracted me from my car, I remember seeing oranges scattered across the road and the truck they came from turned upside down.

The elderly war hero, recipient of a Purple Heart, was dead before his vehicle even hit mine. My knee was decimated, but beyond that, the accident triggered an auto-immune issue that affects my joints, making me feel as old as the man who hit me.

I don't want you to get the wrong idea about me. I'm not bitter. This isn't a *woe-is-me*. I understand that you have to take what life gives you and move on. I'm still here, able to kiss my wife, have a beer, and watch the game—that's a blessing. I complain about the pain from time to time, but I'm thankful for every single day.

Up ahead, I see the usual array of nosey neighbors; they are a fixture at every crime scene. *The looky-loos.* As always, they stand pressed against the yellow crime scene tape, necks craned. Their eyes darting back and forth, determined not to miss a single detail. Most of them are in their pajamas. Several of the women have their hands to their mouths.

They will stand out here all night, just so they can tell the neighbor down the street everything they missed out on, recounting the nitty-gritty as they saw it—the more shocking the details, the better. There is no doubt that tonight's events will feed the gossip mill around here for years.

I duck under the tape, where one of the responding officers is ready to greet me. "Hey there, Parker."

"Hey, Bush." I give him the bro head bob. We move to a safe place, out of the neighbors' earshot. "Okay. Talk to me."

"The victim is Jake Carter. Forty-four years old. He was some kind of big-shot lawyer." Bush refers to his notes. "He lived here with his wife and two teenage children. They were hosting a party here tonight."

"The kids?" I ask.

"No, the parents. The kids weren't home at the time. They are spending the night out with friends."

I look back up the street. "That's why there are so many cars."

"Yep." He flips the page. "Let's see. There were nineteen guests, plus the victim and his wife. Nobody saw anything. You know how that goes."

"I'm afraid I do." I say, tugging at my collar. For May, the air is unseasonably gummy. I can already feel the sweat collecting in the hollows of my body.

Officer Bush goes on to tell me that three guests were permitted to leave the scene—a young man named Greg Prescott, due to a babysitter issue; and also a couple, Molly and George Powell. "The wife had too much to drink. She threw up on the lawn over there." Bush points toward some shrubs. "So they let her husband take her home."

"Did anyone get a statement from them?"

"No. Nothing. They just let them go." My fellow cop gives me an empathetic look. "But everyone else is at the station."

I give old Bush a pat on the back. "It's alright. I'll track them down in the morning." With that, I leave him to maintain the perimeter and push myself up what's left of the hill.

Resting in one of Nashville's most affluent neighborhoods,

the Carter's imposing brick home screams privilege with meticulous landscaping and high-end finishes. A fortress-worthy front door stands open, allowing light from inside to spill out over the lawn. Two grandiose gas lanterns flicker on either side of the entrance. I pull a new pair of shoe covers out of my pocket and slip them on.

Once over the threshold, the ominous feeling from the car intensifies. I do my best to ignore it, but that's a hard thing to do. This hoodoo shit is just something that happens to me sometimes. These doom-and-gloom feelings crop up out of nowhere. I should be better at dealing with them by now, but they rattle me every time.

I take in the scene, finding myself inside a formal two-story foyer. One male victim lies sprawled across the marble tile at the foot of the stairs. There is a decent-sized knife lodged in his chest; his eyes are wide, his mouth hangs open. A single socked foot rests on the bottom step; the ejected shoe lies beside him.

Nothing around the body is disturbed or out of place. The scene isn't bloody. There is no splatter on the wall, and no blood pooled on the floor. The knife has worked like a stopper, keeping most of the blood inside the victim's body. The only blood visible is a bloom of scarlet surrounding the wound. Once Mr. Carter's body has been removed, there won't be anything left to show that a life was taken here.

It's difficult to tell with him in this position, but I'd guess Mr. Carter is pushing 6' 5". He's not only tall but well-muscled. There is no way he saw this coming. His hands are free of defensive wounds. And he should have been more than capable of defending himself if confronted on solid ground.

I think the killer surprised him at the top of the stairs. That's the only thing that makes sense. Mr. Carter would have been off balance without both feet firmly planted. Then the momentum of the blow sent him tumbling backward. I'm not a medical examiner, but I know a broken neck when I see one. If the knife didn't kill him, the fall sure did. I nod my head in agreement with myself and move on to explore the rest of the house.

Opposite Mr. Carter's body, I find a spacious office. Two oversized pocket doors separate it from the foyer. Both doors are slipped almost entirely into the wall. They must be at least ten, maybe even eleven feet tall. I walk between them and enter the room.

The space is oddly murky and shrouded in shadows. I flip the switch with my notepad and have a look around. It's an impressive office. The entire back wall is nothing but books —big, heavy books. A rolling ladder with brass fittings allows access to the highest shelves.

I run my hand along one of two leather club chairs that face a colossal walnut desk standing in the center of the room. The desk is ornate and heavily carved, with what appear to be gargoyles at the top of each leg. I half expect Dumbledore to tap me on the shoulder.

As far as the desk goes, it may hold a couple of clues. I see a trace of white powder on the surface, and one of the bottom drawers is opened halfway. I would be willing to bet a year's salary on what the powder turns out to be. Cocaine is a rich man's drug. For the drawer, I'll leave it for CSI. They will photograph it and dust it for prints before searching the contents.

The desk's companion chair is equally impressive, and instead of passing it by, I'm compelled to sit. The chair is well-worn, but the leather is supple. *Nice ...* and as I sit here, indulging my inner CEO in Carter's fancy chair, the guilt rolls in. I'm enjoying this moment a little *too* much, with the chair's owner lying dead just twenty feet away. *Right. Sorry, man. I'll move on.*

I get my intrusive butt out of Carter's chair, and I'm half-way out of the office when I'm pulled back into the room by a low hum. Curiosity gets the better of me—*it always does*—and I track the buzz to a section of paneling. *Oh my God*, I think it's a hidden door—*a hidden door! I feel like Howard Carter when he discovered King Tut's tomb.*

Giddy to see what's behind it, I give the panel a quick push, and voilà, the door springs open, revealing an elaborate humidor full of cigars. *Not quite as exciting as King Tut, but still pretty cool.* The humidor looks much like a wine fridge—stainless steel with a clear glass door—but intended solely for cigars, controlling the temperature and the humidity.

I open the door and pull out a fat one, bringing it straight to my nose, letting the sweet, loamy smell take me to another place and time, *as smells often do.*

I'm ten years old, sitting on an oil drum in my grandpa's garage, watching him tinker with his prized Thunderbird—a cigar hanging out of his mouth.

That man loved a good cigar. Unfortunately for him, my grandmother did not; whenever Gramps came into the house smelling like cigars, she'd give him hell, prompting Gramps to blame it on someone else. I can still hear him. "I can't help it if the guys at the shop want to smoke cigars, Helen! I don't know what you expect me to do about it!" Then he would throw his hands in the air and huff off—gaslighting Grams just a tad. I take a moment to bask in the warmth of that memory, wishing Gram and Gramps were still around.

I close the door to Tut's tomb and leave the office, glancing over at Carter, almost expecting to see his crooked neck bent in my direction. His wide eyes peering into mine, irked that I was sitting in his chair and touching his cigars. I can feel his dark juju seeping into the soles of my feet and snaking its way through my veins.

Don't ask me why, but this is what happens: every victim stays with me—the good ones *and* the bad ones; I don't get to choose. They climb aboard and lurk inside, waiting for me to fall asleep so they can manifest in my dreams. Each victim is one square of a patchwork quilt that covers me at night when I go to bed, enshrouding me like linen around a mummy. *Ergo, my sleeping problems.*

I have no doubt that Mr. Carter will be stitched in place along with the others by the time my head hits the pillow tonight. I can already feel their bony fingers creeping up my spine, but my ghosts will have to take a backseat for now. I have a job to do.

Beyond the foyer, the house opens up into one palatial, open-concept living space. The seating area and television are to my left, and the kitchen is to my right. A ridiculously long dining room table stretches out between the two. Six upholstered chairs line up on each side, and larger, armed chairs rest on each end. They remind me of thrones.

Do these people really eat here? It seems absurd, but my

mind mocks up a scene. I imagine my wife and I sitting here on our royally pampered asses, one of us on each end, five yards apart.

I would scream from my throne, "How was your day, babe?"

In response, she would yell from hers, "Same old, same old, hon."

Then the two of us would eat the rest of our supper in silence because shouting across the table takes too much effort. *Pfft. Rich people.*

Looking around, it's evident the Carters were entertaining tonight. Abandoned drinking glasses and tiny white plates dot the entire space. Every dish is empty.

That, ladies and gentlemen, is an important clue. *Drumroll, please*—it means the food was good! My stomach gives a niggling rumble, prodding me to act, pushing me toward the kitchen to scope out what's left.

I suppose, if you want to get nit-picky about things, everything in the house is potential evidence. But my victim wasn't poisoned. Thus, this food is irrelevant to the case. And it does look pretty damn tasty.

My stomach pipes up in a growly voice. "It's not something CI would collect anyway, Sol. You might as well enjoy it."

I have to agree. My stomach has a valid point. I snag a fancy-looking shrimp stuffed with what appears to be crab meat and pop it in my mouth, then another two. *Delicious!* While I'm enjoying the food, I take stock of the kitchen.

There is a staggering selection of alcohol presented on the counter, an impressive collection of hard liquors, and, by my count, fifteen bottles of wine. Ten of the bottles are empty or nearly so. I have to accept that most, if not all, of my witnesses will be drunk, or at least would have been drunk at the time of the murder. That stinks. Drunk people make the worst witnesses.

On the upside, I see a knife block missing a single knife. The handles match the one stuck in my victim. *Interesting. A weapon of opportunity? A crime of passion? What happened here?*

I mull it over. There is no way an outsider would have been able to enter the kitchen unnoticed. Not with all these people milling around the food. That means the murderer must have been a guest here tonight. Mr. Carter *invited* his killer into his home. I'm sure of it.

As far as the investigation goes, that's both good and bad. Sure, it's great to have a list with the killer's name on it. You don't get one of those every day. But it's a list with *twenty* names. Each one is likely intoxicated and claiming they didn't see anything. I know I'm in for a long night of endless coffee and evasive witnesses.

Past the kitchen and beyond the butler's pantry, I find a small bathroom and a second set of stairs. The pistons in my brain start firing. If I killed a man at the top of the front staircase, I would wait upstairs until the body was discovered. At that point, the focus would be on the victim in the foyer. Nobody would look behind them to see who was bringing up the rear. Why would they? It would be easy for the killer to come down the back stairs and blend in with the rest of the guests. It's a solid theory and a good plan.

I definitely want to look around up there, but standing here at the bottom, looking up, I decide I'll give the pain pills a little more time to kick in before tackling them. So, I opt to check out the backyard first. I open one of the French doors running along the back of the house and step outside.

The houses in this neighborhood have little space between them, but the lots are deep. And, on this side of the street, they back up to the woods. I note the entire area is fenced-in and well-lit. There is only one gate on the south side of the house. It appears a code is required to unlock it.

I take it all in. Aside from strategic pockets of landscaping, octagonal pavers cover the ground. It's a sweet set-up, perfect for entertaining, with plenty of seating and a cool-looking bar, but it looks like the party stayed inside the house tonight. There isn't a single glass or plate out here. Not surprising with the humidity. I do see a camera that should cover most of the patio. Who knows if it will amount to anything, but it's always worth checking.

Back inside, I nab another shrimp and hoist myself up the back stairs. CI will go through these rooms in detail, but I always like to have a peek for myself. You never know what you might find. Besides, I'm nosey. That's one of the reasons I became a detective. I love a little look-see into people's private lives, turning over their rocks to see what kind of creepy crawlies live underneath.

Up the stairs, I poke my head into a guest room and bathroom. Both are unremarkable except for a hand towel on the bathroom floor. The laundry room is also tidy, with only a few things in the hamper, and the spacious master suite is the same. The king-sized bed is immaculate. There's not a pillow out of place.

One laptop sits on a desk in the corner. CI will process all the computers and phones in the household. It's where people live their lives these days. *And where they keep their secrets.* We all have a few skeletons hiding in our technology closets. *You know it's true ...* Moving on.

I find opposing his and her vanities in the master bath. It's clear which one belongs to the wife. A tray on the counter holds an artfully arranged collection of serums and moisturizers—all in really expensive-looking bottles. I think I'll start with hers.

I tug on a pair of gloves before pulling open the top drawer. Inside, I find several prescription medications with Kimber Carter's name on them—amitriptyline, alprazolam, and hydrocodone. I open the vial with the pain pills. There are only nine. I shake my head, reprimanding myself, and throw it back in the drawer. A fourth, unlabeled bottle contains blue, round pills. I take a photo of the imprint on one of the pills with my cell phone. I'll look that up when I get back to the station.

Several of the remaining drawers contain first aid supplies: antiseptic wipes, assorted antibiotic creams, topical pain relievers, sterile gauze pads, a liquid skin adhesive, and instant ice packs. The sheer amount seems curious, but you never know what you might find in people's bathrooms. I have found a wide array of interesting things. Everything from a super-sized purple dildo to a gorilla costume. Not even joking. True story.

On the other side, Mr. Carter's vanity holds nothing of interest. I find two electric razors, several kinds of hair putty, a super manly-smelling cologne, and a specialized trimmer meant for manscaping. Nothing jumps out at me. His wastebasket is empty, and the lower cabinet holds only fresh towels.

I leave the Carter's bedroom and walk down the hall to the top of the main staircase. The area up here is the same as downstairs; nothing is disturbed. There is no evidence of a struggle. No blood. This murder happened quickly—a stab, a fall, and a death. The entire event took mere seconds from start to finish. *Clean and efficient.* The murderer would have left this scene spotless, without a single drop of blood on them.

The remainder of the second floor doesn't offer much. It consists of a large media room, set up like a home theater, and two additional bedrooms, each with a private bathroom. Everything is pristine—the Carters either have a team of maids or someone with significant OCD issues lives here. It's unnatural for a house to be this perfect.

Outside, I speak with Maddie, the CI supervisor. "Hey, Maddie." I smile, knowing I'm not the only one in for a long night. *Misery loves company.* "It's a big house, clean except for dinnerware from the party. There's a camera in the backyard. Let's pull the video."

I go over the walkthrough in my mind. "I did see a trace of white powder on the desk in the office. I'm thinking cocaine. Also, the bottom drawer of the desk is open. Maybe someone was searching for something. I don't know. It's a stretch, but check for prints." I scratch the top of my head. "Oh yeah, a towel was on the floor in the upstairs guest bathroom. Collect that. I want it tested for DNA. My killer was upstairs at some point."

Maddie nods, and I continue. "The good news is that the weapon came from the household knife block. I'm hoping we can get prints from it. Let me know if anything interesting pops

13

up. You know where I'll be."

"Yeah, I heard there is a whole station full of witnesses to interview! Have a blast staying up all night!" *Ah, her misery loves company too.* She flashes me a light-hearted smile, gathers her kit, and heads for the house.

On the drive to the station, I solidify my theory. The bad guy stabbed my victim at the top of the stairs. *No question.* Carter fell backward, breaking his neck. *Yes. That makes sense.* The killer most likely used the back stairs, either going up or down —maybe even both. *Probably.* He was one of the partygoers and used the victim's own knife to kill him. *I'm convinced.* The only thing I don't have is a motive, and that's a big piece to be missing. I'm hoping something will come out in the interviews.

I skimmed over the list of party guests collected by the officer at the scene. Each guest is named, along with their relationship to the victim. His brother and sister-in-law's names are on the list, along with those of several long-time friends and his business partner. After Mrs. Carter, they are the ones I want to talk to the most. I like to work my way from the victim out, starting with those closest to them.

I was shocked when I recognized two names on the list: Julian Herring and his wife, Susan. Julian's relationship to the victim was listed as *soccer teammate*, along with four other men.

Julian is my insurance broker and has become my good friend. He really helped me out after the car accident. I'll question him, of course, but Julian won't be my guy. He is as mild-mannered as they come. And he's the nervous type, too. *Soccer teammate?* That doesn't sound like Julian at all.

❖ ❖ ❖

At the station, I run background checks on everyone. One of the men, Dan Agee, had a DUI several years ago. Another guest is in the system with an involuntary manslaughter conviction—George Powell. It looks like he got into a bar fight over a woman. Powell spent a year in jail and was on probation for five years.

That was a long time ago, though. He was in his early twenties, and he's been clean since. I look for his name on the list. *Damn.* Unfortunately, he was one of the guests released from the scene. I'll definitely be reaching out to him tomorrow.

I pull my phone out of my pocket and bring up the photo I took at the Carter house of the mystery pill. I plug it into the pill identifier. It is a medication prescribed for ADHD, often misused for its stimulant effects. *I could use one of those tonight.*

Instead, I pour myself a cup of crappy coffee and drink it while watching live surveillance video of Kimber Carter. She sits in an interview room, waiting to be questioned. At one point, she looks straight at the camera. *Wow.* This woman is beautiful. The photos I saw at her house didn't do her justice. She's the kind of woman a man might kill for. *Motive? Maybe.*

CHAPTER TWO

Kimber Carter
MNPD Criminal Investigations Division
Homicide Unit

My mind continues replaying the image of Jake lying dead at the bottom of my beautiful staircase. The scene was shocking, and Jake would have loathed our guests gawking at him in the state I found him. They weren't staring at him because of his perfect, handsome face. Instead, they were repulsed by his twisted, ghoulish one. Yes, there is no doubt. Jake would have hated it to his core.

You must understand. My husband's vanity had no limits. And frankly, for good reason. Women tripped over each other, throwing themselves at Jake. Aside from his beautiful face and well-honed physique, he was successful, wealthy, and charismatic. Those are things every woman wants in a man. Those things drew me in as well.

As far as Jake was concerned, there was no mountain, AKA woman, he couldn't conquer. Everyone was fair game, and over the years, there have been countless affairs. I wouldn't even hazard a guess. It's something we never talked about. *There was so much we never talked about.* I handled it by pretending to be unaware of Jake's transgressions. I turned a blind eye and carried on as if our marriage was perfect.

Looking back now, I can see that Jake chose me because he knew I would accept his behavior. All of it. One day, even the unthinkable—and he was right. Despite everything, I stayed.

For me, our social status was everything. Jake and I were in the upper echelon of Nashville society. We had an image to keep up with. I needed to be on Jake's arm at every formal function, by his side at client dinners, and the woman traveling with him to exotic places full of beautiful people. All of that mattered to me.

And, yes. I do know how shallow that sounds, but those things gave me something to focus on. It's how I've survived. Besides, I didn't care about the affairs. If Jake banged his office aides or pretty waitresses along the way, then so be it. His flings made no difference to me. Lord knows I didn't want to have sex with him. I haven't for a very, very long time anyway. Not since I had my babies. So, I was thankful for the stand-ins. I know that is a strange way for a wife to feel, but there was nothing ordinary about our relationship.

Only once did one of Jake's transgressions upset me. It was when I caught him with Allie, his brother's wife. The memory of that day is crystal clear. It was a Wednesday, and the same as every Wednesday, I was at the Monroe Carell Jr. Children's Hospital. I volunteer as a patient advocate for children whose stay in the hospital will be longer than fifteen days. On that day, though, I wasn't feeling well and left the hospital early.

When I pulled into our driveway, I was surprised to see Jake's flashy sports car parked out front. It was unusual, but on rare occasions, Jake worked from home. Once inside the front door, though, I could see his office was empty.

I was about to call his name when I heard the noises from upstairs. *Those noises—I knew those noises.* How could we keep up with our charade if he brings his sexual follies into our home? Sleep with whoever you want, but not here in the house where I'm raising our children, where we entertain our friends and host our infamous parties.

I climbed the stairs, ready for the scene I knew I would be walking into. The door to our bedroom was open. And there was Jake, in his preferred position at the foot of the bed, pounding away. A few seconds passed before it registered who Jake was defiling this time. It was Allie. *No, not Allie.* Anyone but Allie.

Let's not go through all the sordid details. I screamed. Allie cried. Jake stood by, shrugging his shoulders, looking smug, and gaping at us like we were two hysterical, nonsensical women. In the end, the three of us agreed not to tell Eli. We all knew how much it would hurt him, so it became one more thing that got swept under the rug.

How Jake got Allie upstairs that day, I'll never know. I was sure of her love for Eli. I saw it firsthand. But as I said, Jake usually gets what he wants. He never cared about Allie. He might not have even found her particularly attractive. Jake intended to take something his brother loved and soil it. It's as simple as that.

I wrap my arms around my shivering body. This dreadful

little room they stuck me in feels like a walk-in freezer. Not to mention, it's claustrophobic. I sit here, encased by pallid walls and a single wooden door. The sum decor consists of a small faux wood table with the name *Axel* scratched on its top and two metal chairs. The least the MNPD could do is supply some reading material for their guests as they wait. At minimum a few magazines to flip through. *Disappointing*. I do believe a crypt would have more charm.

When the police transported me here tonight, this is where they brought me, and I have been sitting in here since. Not one single person has been in to check on me. I couldn't even tell you how long it's been. The police asked me to surrender my phone at the house.

I search the walls for a buzzer and notice a little camera in the corner. I lift a finger in the air, hoping that I can get someone's attention. *Hello? Is there someone watching me right now? I would love a glass of wine. Garçon? Un altro vino per favore.* It's not a huge ask. My husband was murdered tonight, after all.

With that, a mushroom of melancholy settles around me. Speaking of wine reminds me of my disrupted party. I can't tell you how disappointed I am that the evening turned out this way. I would like to know what has become of my guests. It is my responsibility to ensure that everyone has a drink in their hand and a smile on their face.

It's almost as though this whole mess is an unexpected extension of the party. *Field trip, everyone!* I clap my hands in my mind. *Let's take a little excursion to the police station. Won't that be fun?*

I know what you're thinking, and I get it. It's not normal.

I'm not normal. But unfortunately, normal has never been my thing. And that fact isn't lost on me either. I'm well aware of my quirks.

Here we have a perfect example. I'm waiting for a detective to come in and talk to me about my husband's murder. And all I care about is my ruined party. At this moment, I can't find any tears for Jake—not a single one.

This whole hoopla, bringing us all to the police station, is a bit much, if you ask me. I understand the police have jobs to do. But as far as I'm concerned, it doesn't matter who the murderer is. Jake will never take another breath. And my life will be better for it.

I'm sure our children will be sad for a time. They do love Jake, but they will continue living their lives. Time will march on, and this ugly event will get farther and farther in the past.

In the interim, I will have to distract them. I'm sure a vacation would do the trick. You know, to get their minds off things. Florence and Venice are spiritual, healing places. Yes. That's what we'll need to put the past behind us and move forward as a family of three.

Those words resonate in my mind, bouncing around before reality hits me. I suck in a sharp breath as I realize everything is mine. All of it—the properties, what's in the bank accounts, stocks, investments, Jake's interest in the firm, and life insurance. *Oh my God, the life insurance.* We have a substantial policy on Jake—several, in fact. A tiny giggle gets away from me. My life is now my own.

Amid my euphoria, the detective enters the room and extends his hand to me. "My name is Detective Parker. I'll be the lead investigator in your husband's murder case." He takes his seat and passes me a water bottle. "First, let me say how sorry I am for your loss. I know this must be a trying time for you. I promise to get you out of here as soon as possible. I understand you've been here for a long time." He strikes me as sincere.

I nod and pat the back of my head, discovering all my hair is still safely tucked away, much like my emotions. I'm sure I look dreadful after all the crying and carrying on I did. Much of it is a blur. The last thing I want to do is talk to this man. Every cell in my body wants to go home. I want to curl up with my fluffy duvet in my comfy bed. A glorious bed, one I no longer have to share.

"Thank you," I say with as much grieving widow sentiment as I can muster. "I am still processing it." I unscrew the cap off the water bottle and take a sip.

He nods. "Let's start at the beginning of the day. Walk me through it."

I sigh for effect. "Well, it was a normal morning. Jake left the house around 6:00 a.m. He usually goes to the gym before work. The kids were spending the night out, as they always do when we have adult parties. So I dropped them off at their friends' houses. After that, I ran a few errands and got home around 4:00 or so."

"You said your children always spend the night away when you have parties. Why is that?"

"We serve a lot of alcohol at our parties. I am more comfortable when they spend the night out."

Detective Parker leans back in his chair. "How much did you have to drink tonight?"

I put my hand to my throat. I do that when I'm nervous. "Oh. Umm … I have no idea." *I'd guess a bottle and a half, maybe two.* "I don't know. A lot, I suppose, along with everyone else." I think back. "Everyone seemed to be enjoying themselves." I perk up, reminiscing about my party, and catch myself smiling. *Stop! Your husband is dead! Grieve Kimber!*

I fill my lungs full of air and hold it, gearing up. The words push out with my breath: "I can't believe he's gone! Oh, Jake!" I put my head in my hands and make exaggerated shoulder movements to simulate sobbing. "Why did this happen?" I wail.

Once I am satisfied I've spent sufficient time weeping, I lift my head and sniff up pretend snot. "I'm so sorry, detective. The grief comes in waves."

Detective Parker narrows his eyes. He opens his mouth to say something but closes it again. I can see the wheels turning. Could it be that I'm not the spectacular actress I imagine myself to be?

"Tell me about your marriage."

"It's fine. We're good." I remember Jake is dead. I correct myself. "We were fine, I mean."

Detective Parker probes. "No problems? No affairs? Nothing at all?"

I take another sip of my water. I need to come clean about Allie. We are all here, and we will all be questioned. I can't afford for the detective to suspect I am hiding anything. "He did have an affair. It was about four years ago, but we dealt with it and moved on. I forgave him."

Parker leans in, interested. "Do you know who the affair was with?"

"Yes." I can hardly bring myself to say it. "It was with Allie Carter."

The detective raises an eyebrow. "Allie Carter? His brother, Eli's wife?"

"Yes, but …." I put both hands flat on the table and plead, "We dealt with it. I forgave both Jake and Allie. Eli doesn't know about it. Please, if there is any way not to bring it up …." My voice trails off.

"Do you think if Eli found out about the affair, he would be angry enough to hurt Jake?"

"No!" My tone is a little too harsh. I take it down a notch. "No. Eli is a good man—a genuinely good man. We all swore not to tell him. Allie is pregnant now, and they are so over the moon about it." My shoulders fall. I'm desperate to save Eli from the truth.

I love Eli. And I was never mad at Allie. "Please," I say. "Please, if you can help it, don't talk to Eli about this." I know it's a childish request. This man has to do his job.

Detective Parker carries on. "Is there anyone else you can think of? Anyone who might want your husband dead?"

Collin, for one. "No," I shake my head, "No one. People always love Jake."

"Have there been any affairs on your end? Any secret lovers? Anything at all?"

"No, there's been no one," I say in truth.

Parker continues to poke. "Your whole twenty-year marriage? In all that time, you never strayed once?"

Why is it so hard to believe? "Never, not even once."

He regards me for a moment and nods his head. I can see he

believes me now. "Okay. Tell me about the party. What was the occasion?"

I look at my nails. I'll need to get a manicure before the funeral—something subtle, maybe a nude. "We never needed an occasion. Jake and I love entertaining. We host parties at our house all the time." With those words, the teeth of anxiety nip me. *Oh no! Will I still be able to entertain? Will they even come to my parties if the magnificent Jake isn't there? I'm feeling panicky. I need one of my relaxers.*

Parker, unaware of my worry, moves on. "I've been to the house and saw all the food. You had your party catered?"

"Yes, we did, but the caterers came and went before the party started."

"Did anything seem unusual with any of your guests?"

"Umm," I go over the evening again and remember something. "Now that you mention it, I do recall seeing Cindy Prescott arguing with her husband. It looked heated." I go on, "They were late to arrive as well."

"Who is Cindy to you?" He asks.

"She is a paralegal for Martin & Carter. I only met her tonight. She's been at the firm for a few months. I believe her husband's name is Greg."

He writes something on his pad and returns to me. "Alright, tell me what made you go into the foyer."

"I hadn't seen Jake for a while. I wondered where he'd gone off to. I thought he might be in his office. So, I went to check, and that's when I saw him lying at the bottom of the stairs." I shudder thinking about how odd Jake looked. "I could tell right away. He was gone." *Collin turned me away.* "I guess I screamed and cried afterward. I don't remember most of it. It's all a bit foggy." I touch the sparkling bracelet on my wrist, Jake's last gift to me. *Unless, of course, you count him dying.*

"Where were you immediately before you went into the foyer?"

I try to recall, "I was talking to one of Jake's teammates and his wife. We were in the living room. Her name was Angela. His name escapes me, but he was a veterinarian." Carter scribbles the name *Angela* and a few other words in his book. I should take this opportunity to shore up my alibi. "I was in the living room for quite a while before I went to look for Jake.

"How long would you say?"

"At least an hour or so. I try to speak with everyone. It's important to me that all my guests feel welcome."

He leans forward. "Did you see anyone going up the back staircase at any time during the party?"

Yes, I did. "No, not that I can recall. Most people know there is a second guest bathroom upstairs. So, it wouldn't be unusual."

"I see." He switches gears. "Did Jake take any prescription drugs?"

"No, never." I can't remember so much as a cold. "Jake was the epitome of good health." I take another little sip of my water, thinking about how Jake's chiseled body will waste away in his grave.

"What about street drugs? Did your husband use narcotics or anything illegal?"

I chew the inside of my lip for a second and decide to tell the truth. "I know Jake kept a small amount of cocaine in his office and some marijuana too." I throw my hands up in defense. "I didn't have anything to do with Jake's drugs. I have no idea how he even acquires them."

"I understand," he hesitates, "I found some medications in your bathroom: anxiety medicine, an antidepressant, hydrocodone, and medication for ADHD. Can you tell me why you have those medications?"

"Oh!" My hand flies back to my throat. I didn't think about strangers going through my private things. "The antidepressants were prescribed to me for sleep." I wave my hand dismissively in the air. "It's an off-label use. The hydrocodone is left over from a dental procedure, and the anxiety medication, "Well ..." I hesitate. I don't even know this man. Collin is the only one who knows about my pills. I clasp my hands and place them in my lap. "I get a little anxious sometimes, and it helps me get over the hump."

He looks at me open, waiting for more. When I give him nothing, he asks, "What causes your anxiety?"

I pause. I don't want to share such personal things with this man, but I carry on anyway. "I'm having a hard time with aging. It's been difficult for me. Every single day, I get older and older. I try to keep up with my looks the best I can, but sometimes I feel the weight of it—the weight of aging." My voice lowers to a whisper. "I have panic attacks about it." Real tears stream down my face, flowing unencumbered for my fading beauty and not a single one for my murdered husband.

Detective Parker looks almost embarrassed but forges on. "And the ADHD medication?"

Again, I choose to tell the truth. "Some days ... I need an extra boost of energy. You know?" Detective Parker nods that he does, and I continue, "It's like a little pick-me-up." I rush to add, "I'm in complete control of it. It's not a big deal." *At least, that's what I keep telling myself.*

His expression has changed to one of pity. "Okay, Mrs. Carter. That's enough for now. Do you have somewhere you can go tonight? The crime scene people will be at your house for a few more hours."

I nod. "My neighbor, Lizzy."

"Alright, I'll interview her next and get you out of here. The detective takes my hand in both of his. "I am so sorry for your loss. I will do everything in my power to find his killer."

You needn't bother. Truly. I manage a little smile. "Thank you, detective. I have no doubt that you will try your very best."

CHAPTER THREE

Lizzy Santos
MNPD Criminal Investigations Division
Homicide Unit

I try unsuccessfully to hide a big, ugly yawn with my hand. We have been sitting in this stale waiting room for, Lord only knows, how long. It all seems a bit excessive. Sure, I get that Jake Carter's murder will be a semi-big deal around here. But still, it's not like he's a legit celebrity or the governor or something like that. Jake was a lawyer, for Heaven's sake. It seems like a lot of fuss. What is that phrase? Ah, yes. Much ado about nothing.

Looking around the room at my fellow captives, I see that half of them are asleep. Poor Allie, bless her heart, is lying across three chairs. It's ridiculous that she has to be here at all. The thought of Allie murdering Jake is absurd. Besides, she is too late in her pregnancy for all this stress. She should be home in bed.

Without thinking about it, I check the time on my phone. I'm startled when the policeman lording over us produces a loud clearing of his throat. *Oh, right.* I forgot we aren't supposed to use our phones. The portly officer raises an eyebrow and shakes his head. *Good Lord.*

I draw in a big breath and sigh, just as loud as our jailor cleared his throat for dramatics. I put the phone back in my lap, but I did get a peek at the time. It's just after midnight. I hope they get to us soon. My buzz is completely gone, despite drinking a whole bottle of wine at the party. And now, all I'm left with are the familiar beginnings of a headache.

Tonight's events were draining. Kimber was hysterical, along with a few of the soccer wives. Someone called 911, and the police cars flew down our quiet street not more than five minutes later. I was shocked to see so many of them. They crawled all over Kimber's front lawn like ants at a picnic.

All the ruckus brought out our neighbors. I swear at least half the neighborhood stood out there, watching as the cops loaded us into the backs of patrol cars. I can only imagine the gossip! I wonder what theories are swirling around about the awful business in the Carter house. It's the most excitement we've had on our street since poor old Mrs. Oshalagel died of a heart attack. She was ninety-eight years old and fell over dead on the way to the mailbox one morning. *God bless her heart and rest her soul.*

The door opens. A middle-aged man calls out, "Lizzy Santos?

"That's me—it's me!" I wave my hand and spring up out of my chair, thankful to be the first of our group called.

He says, "I'm Detective Parker. Follow me, please."

I follow him down a long hall of doors until we arrive at the interview room. He gestures for me to go in. This room is exactly like the ones I see on my true crime shows. I sit in the far chair and feel compelled to speak as the detective takes his. "I'm Lizzy Santos."

He blinks twice, then says, "Yes, I know. I came out and called your name. Remember?"

Oh my gosh, Lizzy! "Oh, yes. Of course. I'm sorry, I'm a little nervous. I've never been in a police station before." I let loose an anxious giggle.

"There's no need to be nervous. I only have a few questions for you, and then we'll get you out of here."

"Okay. Thank you." I study him. He's a little on the thin side, but he has a kind face and lovely green eyes. I sit up a little straighter in my chair and smooth my dress.

"So, Miss," he pauses, "Is it Miss or Mrs.?"

"Oh. It's Mrs." I add, "My husband is out of town. He wasn't able to be here for the party. He's always gone on business, gone all the time, hardly ever home." *Why am I speaking in fragments? Settle down, Lizzy.*

"I got it." Detective Parker winces as he shifts in his chair. "What time did you get to the party?"

"I arrived early, about 6:00. I wanted to help Kimber prepare for the party, but she didn't need much. The caterers were handling the food, and the maid had already been there."

"So, what did you do instead?"

"We talked about our kids. I have a daughter who's almost eighteen. Her name is Chloe, and we talked about what it's like to be the mom of teenagers. Kimber has two: a boy and a girl." I smile. "Do you have kids, detective?"

"I do not." His staccato words tell me he doesn't want me to ask the questions. I put my hands in my lap, waiting for the next question.

"How long have you lived next door to the Carters?"

"Oh, let's see. It has been about ten years."

"And you consider them friends?"

"More like family. Kimber is my closest friend. We get invited to all their parties. And my daughter is allowed to use their pool whenever she wants." Thinking about my sweet girl warms my heart. Words bubble out of my mouth: "She's a water baby for sure, my Chloe; *part fish* is what I always say." It keeps on coming: "She'll be going off to college in the fall." *Quick inhale.* "Her ACT scores were amazing. She was in the top ten percent! Of course, my girl has always been the shiniest star at school. We're so proud of her." I grin at the detective, but his stare is blank. *Shoot, I'm rambling again.* I press my lips together.

"Do you ever socialize with the Carters outside of the neighborhood? For instance, do you go to restaurants together or anything like that?"

"No, not unless you count school events and PTO meetings—you know, those kinds of things. I mostly see her at her house." At this point, I'm confident I have answered his question, but the words flow on anyway. "I've asked Kimber to go to yoga with me a few times, but she always says no. She's one of those women who don't have to work out to keep their girly figure." I slap at my thighs and snort, "Too bad we can't all be so lucky!" *Lizzy, shush!* This poor man looks as tired as I am.

Detective Parker draws in a deep breath. "Did you see anything at the party out of the ordinary?"

"No. I mean, not particularly. I did see Jake having what

appeared to be an argument with Thomas. I'm sure it was nothing. They have a business together. It was probably something about work."

"You couldn't hear what the argument was about?"

I reply, "No, they were outside. I could only see them through the glass."

"Did you start drinking as soon as you arrived?"

"Yes. Only wine, though," I say, as if wine can't get you drunk.

"And Mrs. Carter, was she drinking too?"

I let out a little hoot. "Kimber? Of course!"

Detective Parker shoots me a look. *Lizzy!* "Umm, what I mean to say is, yes. It was a party. Everyone was drinking except for Allie because she's pregnant."

My brain tells me to keep my mouth shut, but I can't help myself. "Allie is out there right now, you know. The poor thing is laid out across three chairs. She could have that baby at any moment! You really should bring her back right away. Stress isn't good for her or the baby." *Another quick breath.* "They're having a baby boy and naming him Liam. I love that name. Don't you, Detective Parker? Babies are so precious! I can't wait to pinch his chubby, wubby, wittle cheeks!" *Oi!* I press my fingers against my lips.

Detective Parker risks asking me another question. "Are you aware of any problems in the marriage?"

Yes. "No."

"Were you aware of any drug use at the party?"

Yes. "No."

"Are you aware of any affairs in the marriage? On either

side?"

Yes. "No."

"Did you ever notice anyone going up the back staircase?"

"I think I saw Collin go up the stairs once, but another guest bathroom is on the second floor. It's not unusual for people to use the one up there. Especially if you have to go number two." I hold up two fingers. His face is flat. I lower my voice. "You know, because the half bath is off the kitchen."

The detective consults his notepad. "Would that be Collin Montgomery?"

"Yes."

"Do you recall when that was?"

Please let this be over soon. "No, I don't remember. I'm sorry."

"It's okay. Can you tell me where you were when Mrs. Carter found her husband's body?" He shifts his weight in his chair from one side to the other and puts his hand over his knee.

"Yes. I was in the kitchen talking to Eli Carter, Jake's brother. Kimber was screaming bloody murder!" As the words leave my mouth, I realize that expression is a little *too* on the money. "Oh my gosh, I shouldn't have said that. It's one of those things that people say when it's not *actually* bloody murder, but this time it is. So, I shouldn't have said that." *Lizzy. Good grief.* "I only meant her screams were ... intense."

"I got it. What did you do when you heard that?"

I turn my palms up. "The same thing everyone else did. We all ran into the foyer."

"Did you notice anyone missing from the group?"

"Not that I can think of. There were so many people at the party tonight. I suppose somebody could have been missing. I do specifically remember Eli, Allie, Collin, and Beth. They were all standing right next to me." I squeeze my legs together. I really need to go to the bathroom.

Parker presses on. "Is there anything else? Something that could help with the investigation?"

"No." I shake my head. "I can't believe this happened. I'm still in shock. I'm not always this … crazy."

"I understand." Detective Parker scoots his chair back and stands. "Mrs. Carter said she could stay with you tonight. Is that right?"

"Yes. Of course."

"Okay, I'll have a deputy drive you both home. If you remember anything that might be pertinent to the case, anything at all, please call me." He hands me his card. I fold it in half and tuck it in my pocket.

"Thank you for your time." He extends his hand.

"You bet!" I say, a little too chipper for the situation. "Can you tell me where the bathroom is?"

He points. "It's the second door on the left."

I give a little smile and make my way to the bathroom. What a night this has been! I take a minute to redo my bun and sort out my dress. Thankful to leave this place, I go to collect my best friend.

CHAPTER FOUR

Kimber: Part One
Day of the Murder

Here I am, teetering on the edge of returning to this world from the ether. I'm aware I was dreaming only a heartbeat ago, but the substance of it is already slipping away. A single breath has passed, and now the memory is lost, like a vapor in the air. Dreams can be fragile that way. Eyes still closed, I let myself continue to drift.

I've always found peace here in the hazy place between dreamy sleep and full awareness, when your consciousness is fluid, traveling effortlessly between the two. I hold on to the feeling as long as I can. It's as if I'm the waves, rolling in and out on the shore, part of the sea one moment and part of the beach the next.

Jake has gone to work, allowing me to roll around and starfish out until my heart is content. I point my pedicured toes underneath the sheets and reach toward the sky. When he's not in the house, I can breathe.

Tonight, we are having one of our parties. A flicker of joy

rolls through me. Jake and I both love entertaining. It's one of the few times we are in sync. It is all a perfectly orchestrated experience.

Our guests will trickle in. I will greet them with all the bells and whistles, as I do. It is of the utmost importance that every guest feels welcomed and attended to. There will be a wide selection of delicious small bites to choose from. Everyone will have a drink in hand and a smile on their face. *Delightful.*

The soirée this evening will be a little different than our usual gatherings. Jake has invited some teammates from his over-forty men's soccer league. They will be accompanied by their wives, of course. It will be good to see some new faces in the mix. Distractions are the best medicine for what ails me. *Along with copious amounts of alcohol and a few pills here and there. But never mind all of that.*

Oh! And I can't forget to call the caterers and confirm the crab croquettes. I know how much Lizzy loves them. Last time, I think she ate them all by herself!

Lizzy Santos is our next-door neighbor. She has lived in the large Tudor-style house for at least a decade with her husband and daughter, Chloe. We don't have much in common other than being moms. To be frank, the woman needs a stylist and fashion consultant. Her clothes are always patterned and painfully colorful. Nevertheless, she is easy to be with, and I can let my guard down around her. That alone means the world to me.

I tick off the things I need to do: drop off the kids, pick up the flowers, and run by the market for lemons, limes, and mint. I also have to make the trek downtown. It's a drive I detest, but a necessary one anyway.

Reluctantly, I leave the comfort of my bed, pad to the bathroom, and ask Alexa for today's weather.

"In Nashville, it's sixty-nine degrees Fahrenheit with cloudy skies. Today, you can expect clouds with a high of eighty-seven degrees and a low of sixty-nine degrees.

I brush my teeth and press on a whitening strip. "Alexa, play my Stapleton playlist."

Alexa replies, "Your Stapleton playlist. From Amazon Music."

My virtual morning companion begins to play my favorite songs while I shower and prepare for the day. My self-care regimen is extensive. I won't bore you with the specifics, but it's the most disciplined part of my day. I've found there is something spiritual in repetition. Having something that you can count on to be the same every day is comforting. So comforting that time flies by.

"Alexa, what time is it?"

She responds, "The time is 8:45 a.m."

Shoot. I need to get going. Before leaving the bathroom, I shake two energy pills from their bottle and peer inside. There are only two left. A wave of anxiety rolls over me and then sits like a rock in my stomach. When I'm low on any of my pills, I get a little panicky.

Please try not to judge me. I don't take energy pills every day. I only take them when I have a lot to do, and today, I have a lot to do. We all have one crutch or another. Let me have mine, and I will let you have yours.

I throw my hair in a ponytail, slip on my favorite black leggings, pair them with a plain white tee, and head downstairs.

In the kitchen, I push the appropriate buttons to make my morning staple—a honey almond milk flat white—80 calories and 2.5 grams of fat. While that's brewing, I check my phone and find three missed text messages from Jake:

Hey, babe, could you pick up my dry cleaning? Thanks! You're the best.
Hey, babe, I think we are out of Hendrick's. Can you grab a bottle while you're out? Thanks! You're a gem!
Hey, babe, don't forget my soccer buddies are coming. Make sure there's enough food. Thanks! XOXO

I put the phone face down and look out onto the patio. We are the great pretenders, Jake and I. He plays the part well, and in turn, I play mine too—the happy wife, the queen to his king. The perfect couple with the perfect life. *What a farce.*

The microwave dings, redirecting my thoughts, and I remove my low-fat blueberry muffin—140 calories and 3 grams of fat. It took me a long time to find a decent muffin that fit within my caloric parameters before I found this winner. It doesn't taste low-fat in the slightest!

While savoring my muffin, a little chirp from the motion sensor tells me that our maid, Maria, is coming through the side gate. As always, she greets me with a genuine smile on her face. I so love that about her—her genuineness.

"Hola, Señora Carter."

"Good morning, Maria." I take a sip of my coffee. "How are you today?"

"Muy bien. Gracias." She sets a basket of conchas on the

counter. "For Cam."

"Oh, thank you so much! Cam will be thrilled."

"No problemo. I know he love." Maria takes an elastic off her wrist and pulls her graying hair back into a bun. She is beautiful in her own right. Even at her age, her olive complexion is flawless.

"I'll be leaving soon, Maria. I need to drop the kids off and run some errands." *Ooooh*. I remember something is coming for me today. "I'm expecting a package. Can you sign for it in case it comes before I get back?"

"Si," another lovely smile, "No problemo. No worry." Maria sets down her tote, a Gucci I gifted her last Christmas.

"Thanks, Maria. I don't know what I would do without you," I say sincerely. She is the glue that holds this place together.

She gathers her supplies and proceeds in the direction of Jake's office. She always starts there. It makes me wonder if she knows about his inky black soul and tries to scrub it out of the room. If she does, it's an exercise in futility. Once Jake touches a thing, it will be stained forever.

After phoning the caterers, I head upstairs to wake my babies. My children hate when I refer to them as babies. I get it. They are nearly grown, but they will *always* be my babies. I don't care how old they are.

Josie is almost sixteen, and our son, Cameron, is fourteen. Like most teenagers, they believe the world revolves around them. Thus, their needs should come before everyone else's. I can remember feeling that way. I suppose we all felt that way once.

I find my son buried under the covers, save for one size

thirteen foot. I grab his toe and tug.

"Hey, Cam, you need to get up." Cam moans. "C'mon, Cam. I have a lot to do today." No response. "I'm going to drop you off at Jacob's. Let's go."

"No, mom. I'm tired." He yanks his foot away from me.

I don't have time for this. "I'm serious!" I jerk the covers off the bed.

"Mom!" He immediately rolls over onto his stomach.

Oh. I sometimes forget my boy is becoming a man. "Cam, I'll go, but you have fifteen minutes to get downstairs. Maria brought you conchas. Make sure you thank her."

I leave Cam and head down the hall. I'm surprised to see that Josie is already up and on her phone when I walk in. "Hey, sweetheart." *Nothing.* I try again. "Listen, I have a lot to do before the party tonight. I want to get out of here in twenty minutes or so. Okay?"

She doesn't even look up from her phone; her thumbs texting furiously. "K, Mom, I'll be down in ten." I recognize when I am dismissed and leave her to it.

My cell phone buzzes in my pocket. I already know it's going to be a text from Collin. It reads—10. I respond with—4. It's something we've done for years. Collin thought it up as a code that tells him I'm okay. The poor thing worries about me every second of every day. It's sweet but unnecessary. I'm *fine*. Sure, I have the occasional breakdown. And I probably drink too much, but neither is anything new. You would assume that after all these years, he would have gotten used to it.

◆ ◆ ◆

By some miracle, the kids and I are loaded and ready to go in my black SUV right on schedule. Josie is riding shotgun, a perk of being the oldest child; her earbuds are in, her bare feet are on the dash, and her flip-flops shed on the floorboard. One foot is tapping along with whatever she's listening to. The air conditioning is blowing her highlighted hair away from her face.

I see the woman inside her more each day. In two short years, she'll be gone, backpacking through Europe with her friends, doing the whole *gap year* thing. They will be living their lives and discovering their passions. It's all she talks about since her father agreed she could go. I pushed hard for it. *Spread your wings, my little dove, and fly far away from this place.*

My greatest fear has always been that my precious girl would inherit my madness. I've been vigilant, looking for even the slightest sign that something is amiss. Thankfully, all I've seen is run-of-the-mill teenage antics with a touch of rebellion.

I've seen no hints of self-destructive behavior—no scars, no screaming, and no blood. Josie is a well-adjusted, confident girl, and I couldn't be more thankful that she is nothing like me.

I take a peek in the rearview mirror at Cam. He's focused on his video game, his dark hair obscuring his face, utterly clueless about how much I love him. He looks so much like his father, but that's where their similarities end. Cam is loving and kind. I've never worried about him the same way I have with Josie. My *disease* has always felt like a female affliction.

I need to hold on until Cam is out of the house. He will be going to Austria to study for his senior year. I will miss my children more than I can say, but I am having trouble hanging on these days. I don't want them to watch as their mother completely loses herself. I've been able to keep all the scary bits of my life hidden, but I don't know how much longer I'll be able to pull that off.

CHAPTER FIVE

Collin

Four Days Before the Murder

It's Monday night. I know Jake is out of town, and the kids are out of the house spending the night with friends. That means Kimber is home alone. She tends to go off the rails when she has the house to herself without anyone to masquerade for.

I texted her over an hour ago, and she still hasn't responded. Now, impatient, I'm going to call her. So much can go wrong in an hour. The call is picked up, but I only hear mumbling on the other end. I grab my keys and fly out the door. Kimber. *I'm coming. Hang on.* I don't tell Beth I'm leaving. I don't have the time to argue about it.

I find Kimber lying naked on the bathroom floor—eyes closed, cell phone in her hand, and blood everywhere. Shards of glass and cotton balls cover the tile. It is a variation of a scene I know too well. I can feel the glass crunching under my shoes as I kneel beside her. Brushing the hair out of her face, I try to rouse her. "Kimber? Kimber, I'm here. Wake up."

Her eyes flutter open, and she says only, "Collin," before closing them again.

I take her face in my hands, wiping a tear away with my thumb. "Kimber, this is important. Was it only wine tonight, or did you take some of your relaxers?"

"Just drink," she murmurs without opening her eyes.

Thank God. "Okay," I know the routine. "We need to get you cleaned up and find out where all this blood is coming from." My eyes sweep over the length of her beautifully perfect body. Her thighs, stomach, and breasts are smeared in scarlet. I find a decent-sized gash on her foot, likely an accident, and several on her thigh. Those are *not* accidents. There are also little cuts on both her hands and feet.

Bits of glass stick to her skin, glued on with dried blood. I pick them off one by one. "What happened tonight, Kim?" I whisper, more to myself than to her, even though I know the answer. She hates who she is. She can't help herself.

I start the bath and gather the large pieces of the shattered jar. Kimber moans when I lift her off the floor. I lower her into the warm water and begin to wash away the evidence of her pain. Her head is thrown back, exposing her throat. Her arms float on the water's surface.

I squeeze the water—now blushing with her blood—out of the washcloth and watch it cascade over her nipples. I would bet my life Jake has never done this once. She would never be this honest with him, this raw. You are only this vulnerable with the people you know will love you no matter what.

When I have finished bandaging her wounds, I call Beth. She answers on the first ring. "Collin?"

"Hey Beth, listen, I had to check on Kimber. Jake is out of town again, and she is having a rough night. She's okay, but I should stay the night." Her silence speaks volumes on the other end, but I continue. "She's sleeping now, but she's in a bad way. I don't want her to be alone."

Barely audible, Beth replies, "Okay."

"I love you, Beth. I'll see you in the morning." I hang up the phone, feeling that familiar pang of guilt. It comes every time I choose Kimber over my wife. Nonetheless, I take my place next to Kimber tonight, breathing every breath with her.

◆ ◆ ◆

The early morning sun wakes me. I look over at Kimber, still sleeping, still breathing—last night was scary for me. When she didn't respond to my texts, I thought the worst.

It's not the cutting. That's not the scary part. I've dealt with that for a long time. I know that isn't about trying to take her life. The cutting is about being overwhelmed with emotion and needing an outlet. I hate that she does it, but I have come to accept it and even understand it, at least a little bit. The scary part is that Kimber has added pills to the mix. One wrong combination, and her life—our life—would be over. She'd slip away in the smoky haze of intoxication. Closing her eyes and then forgetting to breathe, leaving me behind.

Looking at her sleeping now, no one would know anything about the turmoil boiling over inside her. Her self-loathing. Her worst memories. Her desperation for answers. Kimber wears a mask for everyone, sometimes even me.

There was a time when the turmoil settled, like sand on the ocean floor, allowing her to see the world through a new lens. When her kids were little, Kimber was the happiest I had ever seen her. But something changed a year or so after she gave birth to Cam. I considered postpartum depression, but my gut told me it had something to do with Jake. Whatever it was, catapulted Kimber back to drinking daily. This go-round, she chose wine instead of vodka as her poison.

One day, I confronted her about it. "I need you to tell me. What has Jake done, Kimber? I know you. I know when you're struggling. Please talk to me."

"Don't be ridiculous, Collin. I'm fine. I'm always fine. You know that." Kimber clucked, dismissing me with a wave of one hand while holding a glass of wine in the other.

"You're not fine, Kimber. It's Jake, isn't it? Is he having an affair?" She has always hidden the details of her life with Jake from me. Most likely, for my own sake. I keep pushing. "Whatever he's done, you don't have to stay with him. You could leave."

"Oh, Collin. Don't be so obtuse. Jake has had affairs since the beginning. I don't care, better them than me. You know how I feel about sex."

"Kim, you deserve better than that." I reached out and put my hand on her knee. "You always have."

"Do I?" She laughed.

"This isn't funny, Kimber. Something is wrong, or you wouldn't have started drinking again."

47

"Collin, I'm not getting into this discussion with you. If it bothers you to see me drinking, don't come over."

Before I could say anything else, Jake strode in. "Hey there, buddy. How's it hanging?" He slapped me on the back and bent to kiss Kimber on the forehead.

I left that day with fresh wounds. Kimber's words echoed in my head: *Don't come over.* Those words stung and sent me flying back to the past. Back then, whenever we fought, Kimber threatened to leave me. She swore she would go back to her parents' house, as if she could go on with or without me. I drove around for hours to shake it off before going home. I can't go home to Beth, upset about Kimber. It isn't fair to her.

Anyway, I've watched her regress over the years. The old Kimber has crept back into her skin. She is better than ever at hiding it. But her demons have come home to roost. I don't know what Jake's done, but I know he's responsible.

Kimber rolls onto her stomach and moans lightly. My eyes trace her spine, following it down the middle of her back. Halfway down, I stop short. I can see a bruise peeking out from underneath the sheet. I pull back the covers and see Kimber colored in shades of purple and green. Bruises run from the middle of her back to halfway down her thighs. I know she didn't do this to herself.

Last night, when I lifted her out of the tub, I laid her on the bed, drying her front and tending to her wounds. I did notice a few bruises, one on each knee and one on her shoulder, but I didn't think anything about them. Kimber gets drunk and stumbles around. Any bruises I saw over the years, I chalked up to that. But these aren't from bumping into something or an accidental fall. And she sure as hell didn't run into something dozens of times while walking backward.

Jake did this—Jake did this to her, and I'm going to kill him. A rush of adrenalin runs through me. I have always hated Jake, but I won't stand by and let this happen. I need to figure out what I'm going to do. There is no question that something has to be done. I don't have a plan yet, but this will not stand, no matter the cost.

I look at the clock. *Crap.* I'm supposed to be at a parent-teacher meeting with Beth in an hour. I don't want to wake Kimber, so I leave a note.

Kimber, we need to talk. XXOO

◆ ◆ ◆

Kimber
11:36 a.m.

I surface into consciousness with a very vague memory of last night. I'm clean. I'm in bed. So I know Collin was here. As I rise to get out of bed, the familiar pain from an episode screams at me from behind. *Shit.*

If Collin was here, then he knows. I close my eyes and lie back down. Collin was never supposed to find out. I have avoided this very thing for years and years. It's been one of my best-kept secrets, and now one night and a lapse of judgment have put me in a terrible predicament.

I force myself to get up. I take three pain pills, break them in half, and swallow them with a glass of water. I want to get this conversation with Collin over with. The sooner, the better.

I send him a text:

Hey, Collin. Thanks for last night. Can you come over ASAP? I know what you want to talk about. It's not what you think. I promise.

He responds immediately:

I can be there in an hour, but don't think you can bullshit me, Kimber.

I'm on the patio, taking in the early afternoon sun, awaiting Collin's arrival. I know what I have to do. I need to be convincing, matter-of-fact, and steadfast. Jake hurts me because I want him to. That's my story, and I'm sticking to it.

I hear Collin's truck pull into the driveway and ready myself. A minute later, he comes through the side gate, walking toward me, looking like the weight of the world is on his shoulders. "Hey, Kimber." He takes the chair next to me. "Are you okay?"

I prepare, "Collin, I'm fine. This isn't the first time I've had a hangover." I study him through my sunglasses. He's clenching his jaw. That's never good.

"You know that's not what I'm talking about." He pauses, "Kimber, the bruises."

I take a sip of wine. "I know what you're thinking, but you're wrong. I am not being abused. I am being satisfied. It's something that has been a part of my sex life with Jake from the very beginning. That's why I slept with him more than once, unlike all the others."

"I don't believe you, Kim." His voice is solemn.

"Collin, it doesn't matter if you believe me or not. It's the truth." *Lies. Lies. Lies.* "Jake only does what I ask him to."

"Kimber, what I saw was not a little slap and tickle. What I saw looked like a beating. A *brutal* beating."

I roll my eyes. "They look so much worse than they are. I'm telling you the truth. You don't need to worry. Nothing has changed. I never shared this part of my life with you because I knew you wouldn't like it. But Jake and I are consenting adults, and what we do in the bedroom is nobody's business but ours."

His face is pained with frustration. "No man who loved you would be able to do that. I know you have issues, Kimber, but this is too much." He shakes his head and says, "Even if you want it, I still hate him for it."

Okay. Maybe he believes me. I relax a little. "Collin, you would hate him no matter who he was or what he did to me." *First lies, and then distractions.* "Can you stay around for a couple of hours? I thought we could order pizza and watch a movie like old times. Jake won't be home until late."

Collin's face softens. "Yeah. I can stay, but I get to pick the movie."

I'm right there with him. "Only if I can pick the toppings!"

He points at me, then, with a drawl, he says, "You've got yourself a deal, little lady."

My hands go to my head as if I'm preparing for an assault. "Oh, Lord. Does that mean we are watching a Western?"

Keeping in character, he says, "You can bet your pretty little boots we are." He reaches for my hand. "How 'bout we mosey on inside and order us some grub?"

I take his hand, and at that moment, it feels like we are teenagers again. Me and Collin against the world.

CHAPTER SIX

Eli
MNPD Criminal Investigations Division
Homicide Unit

A slender, mild-looking man stands in the doorway and calls Lizzy's name. She springs out of her chair as if she has discovered the golden ticket. I look at my pregnant wife, hoping we will be next. Allie is exhausted. She's taking up three chairs and sleeping across them as a makeshift bed. She can't be comfortable lying on these hard plastic seats three weeks from her due date.

If I was in my right mind, I would have gotten Allie to say she was having contractions. We could have avoided this shitshow altogether, but my mind was firing in a million different directions. Between digesting what happened with Jake and the bourbon in my system, I wasn't exactly on my game.

I file through the things to do. I'll have to call my parents and tell them their firstborn son is dead. *Crap.* That's going to suck.

I'll need to book their flights. Otherwise, they will call a travel agent. I have tried, over and over, to explain how easy it is to book flights on the computer. But they don't want to hear it.

My father said, "Son, those machines are taking good jobs away from men and women trying to make an honest living." He raised a finger in the air, "Mark my words. Computers will be the downfall of humanity!"

I guess that's not the craziest thing anyone has ever said.

I've decided to wait until the morning to tell them what's happened. There's no use waking them from a sound sleep with news that will throw my mother into hysterics. Waiting a few hours won't change anything. Jake will be as dead in the morning as he is right now. You won't see me shed a tear for him, but I know my mom will cry rivers.

The scene plays out in my mind. The house phone will ring in my parents' Punta Gorda, Florida, home. They still have a landline, just one phone attached to the wall in the kitchen. My mom will shuffle to the phone in her fuzzy slippers and housecoat. Dad will be at the kitchen table. He will be reading the newspaper. A bowl of cornflakes topped with a diced banana will sit before him.

I'll ask Mom to speak with my father so he can be the one to break it to her. I sure don't want to be the one. Dad will keep it together for Mom's sake, although I know how crushed he'll be when I tell him that his favorite son, his golden boy, was cut down in his prime. They were both so proud of Jake's successes. And now all they have left is me, the lackluster, very mediocre son.

Of course, we will have to make all the funeral arrangements. I want to help Kimber with those things, but I have no idea if Jake wanted to be cremated or buried. If I had to guess, I bet Jake wanted a marble mausoleum, complete with a gilded statue of his likeness standing at the door. *Whatever.* Let's build him an effing monument and get it over with.

I know that sounds harsh, but Jake doesn't deserve any sympathy—not from anyone. I have wished him dead a thousand times. I even imagined the different ways it could happen. Now that it's a done deal, I'll be free.

All that being said, as much as I hate it, there is a pestering twinge of something at the back of my mind. It feels something like worry, but not exactly. I can't stop thinking about Jake's body—my brother's *actual* flesh and blood body. Is it still lying there on the tile? Is it stiff yet? Has lividity set in? How long will it be on the floor like that?

If the TV crime shows are anything to go by, his corpse will lie there for hours while crime scene analysts take pictures and do all their crime scene things. I think, at some point, the coroner has to come to the scene. Jake could be lying there for hours. It makes me mad that I even care. I know I shouldn't. Jake was an awful human being. *He was the worst brother ever, Eli. He doesn't deserve a fleck of pity. Move on.*

My mind turns to Kimber. I have always wondered how she could tolerate his astronomical ego and infidelity. After what happened with Allie, I thought she might leave him, but she stayed. It was as though nothing had ever happened. I decided she must have held on to the marriage for the children. *But those screams.* Is it possible they had real love there? *No.* Kimber may have loved my brother, but Jake only loved himself, his fortune, and the spotlight. He was incapable of anything else.

The door swings open again, and an officer appears, followed by Lizzy and Kimber. Lizzy has her arm around Kimber, who is looking at the floor. Lizzy makes eye contact with me and gives me an empathetic smile.

"Eli Carter?" The detective calls my name with a cup of coffee in his hand.

I hate leaving Allie while she's sleeping and debate whether I should wake her. I decide against it. She looks peaceful, believe it or not. I look to Collin. He nods. I know he will take care of her in my absence.

The detective directs me to a small room. I take the seat farthest from the door.

From the doorway, the detective asks, "Can I get you some water or coffee?" He raises his cup.

"No, thanks." I say, waving him off, "I'm good."

"Okay." The detective shuts the door and groans softly as he takes his seat. This guy looks even worse than I feel. And that's saying something. "Let me start by saying that I'm sorry for your loss. I understand this must be a difficult time for you." His sympathy feels genuine. "You are his younger brother?"

"Yes." I rub the stubble on my chin. It's more than a five o'clock shadow at this point. "We are four years apart. I mean, were."

"Are there any other siblings?"

"No, it was just the two of us."

"Okay. I'm Detective Parker. I will be the one handling your brother's case." He opens his notebook. "I will try and be as brief as possible. I know it's been a long night."

I bob my head. "Thanks."

"What time did you get to your brother's house tonight?"

I try to remember. It feels like so long ago. "I think it was around 8:00."

"What did you do when you arrived?"

"I got a drink. Allie wasn't drinking, of course, because she's pregnant."

Parker scratches something in his book. "What was the general mood of the party?"

What the hell does that even mean? "I guess you could say upbeat. Everyone seemed to be having a good time. People were conversing and laughing. The median age was about forty-five, so it wasn't a banger or anything."

"I see. Did anything unusual happen at the party? Did you notice anything out of the ordinary?"

An unexpected burst of anger bubbles out. "Besides my dead brother with a knife in his chest?" *Eli, keep it together.* I immediately hold up my hand and say, "I'm sorry. I didn't mean …." *Just breathe.* "It's been a long night. And as you know, very stressful." I start over. "So, to answer your question, no. I didn't see anything unusual before that."

"Do you know if there were any problems in your brother's marriage?"

How should I answer this? "As far as I'm aware, they were okay."

Parker pushes. "Are you aware of any affairs?"

He's going to ask about Jake and Allie. Kimber must have told him. I don't want to talk about this. *Shit.* "I know he had one years ago."

"Do you know who it was with?"

God damn it. "I do." *I hate this so much.* I take a deep breath and say my wife's name. "Allie. It was with Allie."

Parker's eyes are fixed on me. "And when did you find out about it?"

"Allie came home the same day Kimber found them together and confessed to me. I forgave her. We put it behind us." I press my hands in front of me. "It's a non-issue. Honestly, we moved past it."

Parker rubs his forehead. I don't think he believes me. "Did you ever confront your brother?"

"No. Our relationship was complicated."

"Did you hold any resentment toward your brother for that?"

My hands curl into fists. I can't help but raise my voice. "Would you hold resentment if your brother screwed your wife?"

The detective looks me evenly in the eye. "Hell, yeah! I'd want to kill him!"

I feel like I'm losing control here. I take a beat to compose myself. "Look, this happened over four years ago. I forgave Allie, and we moved on. If I was going to kill Jake over it, I would have done it back then." I huff in frustration. "I get that you have a job to do, but I promise you, you're barking up the wrong tree."

Parker takes a sip of his coffee, allowing the stress level in the room to come down a few pegs. "Okay, can you tell me where you were when your sister-in-law discovered your brother's body?"

"I was in the kitchen talking to Lizzy. She's Kimber's neighbor." I remember Lizzy has been in here. "You probably already know that." I wonder if Kimber told Lizzy about Jake and Allie.

Parker carries on. "How long were you in the kitchen with Mrs. Santos before going to the foyer?"

"Ten or fifteen minutes."

"And where were you before that?"

"I was talking with my wife, Collin, and his wife, Beth, in the living area."

The detective leans back in his chair. "Why did you leave the conversation and go to the kitchen?"

"To make another drink. I was drinking bourbon. Lizzy was sitting at the island, and we started chatting." I slump in my seat a little and stretch out my legs. My back is killing me, and my head is pounding. I want to get the hell out of here.

"Do you remember what the two of you were talking about?"

I rub my stubble again. I'll have a full beard before long. "We were talking about the food—that it tasted good or something along those lines."

"Are you aware of any drug use at the party?"

I remember the fat bag of weed in my pocket. "Jake does blow sometimes, but I don't touch the stuff."

"Did you happen to see anyone go upstairs while you were there?"

Yes, I saw Jake go up the stairs. "No. No one."

"How about you? Did you go upstairs?"

Only once. "No. I didn't." I'm surprised by how easy lying comes to me.

"If you had to guess," Parker taps his pen on the table, "who at the party would have wanted your brother dead?"

I turn up my palms. "The only difference between tonight

and all the other parties are the soccer guys. I'd look at them. Jake always talked shit about his game. You know, bragging like he was the star of the team." I offer, "I wouldn't be surprised if one of them got pissed off and did something about it."

"Did you ever attend any of your brother's soccer games?"

"No, not one."

"So, tonight is the first time you have met any of your brother's teammates?"

"Tonight is the first night I have ever *seen* them," I say, trying to stretch my legs out even further, "but I still haven't *met* any of them. They stayed to themselves all night. I thought they seemed like a bunch of assholes."

"What makes you think that?"

"They were all like little Jake juniors. Big egos and loud mouths."

The detective studies me. "Why did you continue to socialize with your brother after what he did?"

"It was hard, but Allie and I love Kimber and those kids. I wasn't going to let what happened keep me away forever. We stayed away for a while, but our relationship with the kids brought us back."

Parker scribbles a couple of words in his notebook. "Okay, Eli, let's go get your wife. I promise to be brief."

He leads me back out into the waiting room. I can see Allie is still sleeping. I crouch next to her. "Al? Al, it's your turn." She rouses, disoriented. "Allie, it's your turn to talk to the detective, and then we can go home."

"Mmmm. K." She sits up but still seems out of it. I help her stand and hand her off to Detective Parker.

There is no doubt he will ask her about the thing with Jake. I hate that the memory of those moments with Jake will even flash through her mind. It makes me sick. *Screw Jake.* I don't feel guilty about anything. The son of a bitch got exactly what he deserved.

CHAPTER SEVEN

Kimber: Part Two
The Day of the Murder
10:04 a.m.

Having dropped my children off at their friends' houses, I'm alone in my car, singing along to Jason Aldean's Crazy Town. The area I have to go to is a little seedy, as you might expect it to be when buying illicit drugs. It's a trip I hate making, but that hasn't dissuaded me yet.

After driving down here the first time, I did consider buying a gun to protect myself. But I couldn't see myself carrying one around, let alone pointing it at someone and pulling the trigger. So, in the end, I settled on pepper spray. I guess it's better than nothing.

I bet you're a little shocked to know that I'm on the way to visit a drug dealer. I could have never imagined it myself not so long ago. I'm not proud of it, but we all have our secrets, don't we? This little drug thing is only one of many for me, and it's not even the worst.

This whole thing began when another mom told me where she got all her energy. Sarah Miller, the other mom, and I were on the PTO together. She was the classic supermom. I marveled at how she volunteered for everything and came through with what she promised. Meanwhile, I struggled to deliver store-bought brownies to the bake sale.

"Where do you find the energy for all of it?" I asked one day.

Supermom paused and said, "I take a supplement. It's amazing."

"You mean like a vitamin? What kind of supplement?" *Whatever it is, I need it.*

She looked around and lowered her voice. "It's a prescribed medication. The doctor wrote my son a prescription for his ADHD. But my son didn't like the feeling the drug gave him. I knew it helped with focus and energy, so I tried one out of curiosity. That day, I cleaned my whole house. I don't think it's ever been so clean. After that, I kept refilling his prescription. Only, I'm the one who takes them."

My mind immediately went to work. Could I get one of the kids diagnosed? *No.* They were already too old for that. I figured you could buy them on the street, but I had no idea how one goes about finding a drug dealer. I went through all the people I came into contact with who might know where I could get some: the pool guy, my mechanic, the gardener, the leery-eyed man at the dry cleaners. *Who?*

I mentioned it in passing to various people. I'd say, "I need something to give me more energy," hoping someone would offer the right suggestion. "If only there were a pill I could take …."

Finally, I got the response I was looking for from the girl who worked part-time at one of my favorite lunch spots. She was a college student, pre-med if my memory serves me—a cute little blonde thing.

"Actually," the blonde thing said, tapping her pen to her cheek, "I do know a guy." She explained that some students take pills to stay up all night while cramming for exams. "I can get you his number." She left and came back with the bill and a phone number. "Just say you're a friend of Anna's, and tell him what you need."

"Thanks!" We traded smiles, and I watched her bop away. She was so fresh. *I was that fresh once.* I couldn't help being jealous of her youth. There's nothing wrong with that, is there? I mean, who wouldn't choose to be younger if they could? I would do anything to get my eighteen-year-old body back!

Anyway, I deposited a one-hundred-dollar bill in the folder—twenty for the meal and eighty for the information. Part of me felt like I had already committed a crime simply by having this man's number, but I went straight to my car and made the phone call anyway.

The voice on the other end answered with a "Yo." I explained what I needed and set up my first pickup. That was four years ago, and ever since, I have made the pilgrimage to get the goods every couple of months. As I said, the dealer's neighborhood is sketchy. It's spattered with abandoned houses and overgrown yards. Every stop sign is covered in graffiti.

The worst part is that people are always hanging around outside. Mostly men. I try not to make eye contact with anyone. I stare ahead and act like I belong down there, hoping that I'll be left alone. It's worked for me so far.

I make the left turn down Killa's Street and pull in front of number 1152. I honk three times, signaling he has a customer. The house is a tiny white two-story with a slanted wooden porch and a dark green roof. A box air conditioner hangs out the top window, and a Doberman barks at me through the chain-link fence.

The front door swings open, and Killa, not his God-given name, I assume, saunters out. His basketball shorts hang off his bony hips, exposing a pair of checkered boxers. A pair of bright yellow high-tops adorn his feet, and a long gold chain hangs on his neck. No shirt; only a small patch of hair in the middle of his chest.

He looks around. I presume to check for police or even drug-dealing rivals. Once he determines the coast is clear, Killa yanks up his shorts, adjusts his crotch, and heads my way. I lower the passenger side window, allowing his pockmarked cheeks and scraggly goatee to fill the space. He peers in and flashes his golden teeth.

We don't speak to each other. We've done this plenty of times. It's always the same. I give him four hundred dollars. Killa hands me a baggy containing forty pills. Our negotiated deal. I have no idea if I'm overpaying or not, and I don't care. I'm happy to have survived this transaction once more. I pull away from the curb, anxious to leave 'Scary Town' with my windows up and doors locked. Luckily, it's not too far off the freeway. Once I make it into the flow of traffic, I relax.

I continue to do the rest of my errands. The first stop is the liquor store for extra wine. You can never have too much wine, you know. And I need to pick up Jake's favorite gin. Then I'll be on to the florist, the grocery store, and the dry cleaners.

Driving down the road, I'm annoyed to see my husband's dashing face smiling at me from a billboard. This one must be new. It wasn't here the last time I came this way. Sometimes, I change my whole route so I don't have to pass by his perfect, toothy smile. At this rate, there will be no safe roads for me to drive on. I crank the radio for distraction and forge ahead, longing for a relaxer and a glass of wine.

◆ ◆ ◆

4:18 p.m.

My errands done, I pull into the driveway and begin to unload the car. It takes me several trips. I may have overdone it at the liquor store, but I'd rather have too much than not enough—*that's a rule I live by*.

Before anything else, I need to get these beautiful flowers into water. I choose three large ironstone jardinières: a tall one for the foyer table and two short, wide jars for the coffee tables. I cut the stems to length, and after adding some greenery from our garden, I stand back to admire my work. *Gorgeous*. I have to admit that I have a knack for it.

The thing about fresh flowers is that, in the beginning, they are so lovely and fragrant, but they don't last. The moment they are past their prime, the very second their beauty begins to fade, I have to throw them out. Jake has no tolerance for imperfection when it comes to anything, so neither do I.

I unpack Jake's gin, all the other booze, and the extra wine. I can see Lizzy's daughter, Chloe, swimming in the pool. She's a beautiful swimmer with such elegant lines. I watch her for a few minutes, but I need to get ready. My goal is to be finished upstairs before Jake gets home. I jog up the back steps, and the smell of fresh linen fills the air. Maria is in the laundry room, folding. "Hello, Maria. How's everything going?"

Maria smiles as she folds my towels. "All downstairs finish, your room too. I still have finish this laundry and kids' room." Her English has improved so much since she started working for us, but she still has a ways to go.

"Sounds good," I toss words behind me as I head toward the bedroom, "I'm going to be getting ready."

Maria calls back. "Si, okay. I put package on sink."

Squealing like a little girl, I hurry to my bathroom, thrilled about my order from Tiffany's. I tear through the packaging and open their trademark blue jewelry box. It's exquisite and looks even better in person than it did online.

I remove my treasure from the box to admire it. The 18kt gold bypass bracelet is breathtaking, featuring a ball on each end, one polished gold and the other encrusted with brilliant round diamonds. I love it!

I always buy myself a treat after one of Jake's episodes. He never complains about the money spent, and honestly, it helps me get through. I throw the wrapping in the garbage can and put several tissues over the top. Jake has never said anything about the money, but that doesn't mean I should poke the bear. *Better safe than sorry—another rule I live by.*

It's time to deal with my contraband. I pull the baggie with the pills out of my purse and transfer them to an unmarked bottle. I always feel a sense of relief when my bottles are full. Comfort comes with the knowledge that the pills are there if I need them.

When I first started bringing home these ill-gotten drugs, I hid them inside a boot in my closet. Skulking around like some secret operative on a classified mission. Thinking back now, it seems so silly. Jake never went through my drawers, and the kids had no reason to. Did I care if Maria saw them? No, I decided. I did not. So now they live with my other pills in my vanity drawer.

"Alexa, what time is it?"

She responds, "The time is 4:55 p.m."

I peer at myself in the mirror, checking for new lines or wrinkles. It's a daily exam, making sure my teeth are white enough, my skin smooth enough, my lips full enough, and for the moment, I pass.

I put on light make-up—only the basics—mascara, eyeliner, *top lid only*, light blush, eyebrow pencil, and lip gloss. Jake prefers me this way, and I must produce whatever he expects. Even though sometimes I don't know what that expectation is until it's too late.

Now, with my face done, I take tonight's dress off the rack and remove the plastic. *Gorgeous.* I buy a new dress for every party, and this time it's a sleek black pencil dress from one of my favorite designers. I grab a pair of black kitten heels off the shelf and slip them on.

Every woman knows that how you feel about yourself can make or break an evening. An ill-positioned pimple can ruin the whole night. *This night,* I feel good about myself.

Pleased with my dress, I throw my hair into a French twist, securing it with an antique comb purchased in Greece last summer. I'm careful to tuck every hair in place. A tidy updo is a must. That particular violation has gotten me in trouble more than once. After a liberal amount of hairspray, I grab my bracelet and leave our bedroom just in time. As I am treading down the back stairs, I hear Jake bounding up the front.

I compile all the booze and mixers for the party on the counter. I go through everything: club soda, simple syrup, tonic water, cherries, mint, olives, cola, and ginger ale. *Check.* Next, I line up the barware. There are wine, cocktail, highball, and rocks glasses. After confirming the glasses are evenly spaced, I fill the ice buckets. Finally ready, I pour myself a generous glass of pinot noir and begin cutting the lemons and limes.

Maria comes into the kitchen. "All done, Señora."

"Thank you so much, Maria. The house looks great, as always," I say, cutting into a lemon. "I'll see you in the morning. Si?"

"Si. Mañana." She gathers her bag and leaves out the back. Usually, she doesn't come on Saturdays, but we pay her double to work the day after one of our parties.

As I'm washing the knife and cutting board, I hear the front door open, followed by Lizzy calling, "Hello?"

Lizzy always comes early, offering to help set up for the party. Of course, she knows there is never anything to do.

We have hosted countless parties. She knows that our evening parties are *always* catered. She also knows that we have a maid.

Lizzy comes here early because she is bored stiff at her house, and I imagine it *is* lonely over there. All she has is Chloe. John is never home, and I don't know what keeps her busy all day besides cleaning her house, the occasional yoga class, and Law and Order. I don't mind her pretending, though. It's something I understand well. In fact, I'm thankful she comes early. It gives me a little time to breathe before the party starts.

"Back here, Lizzy," I call.

She enters the kitchen wearing another incredibly colorful dress. Circles of bright orange and lemon yellow pop out on a cream background. It reminds me of Easter. I can't help but wonder if she chooses outfits like this to distract people from her very average face. *I know! I'm horrible. I'm sorry, but it's true.*

Lizzy pours herself a glass of wine and takes a stool at the island. I make a plate of cheese and crackers, and we settle into our usual, uncomplicated dialogue.

My cell phone buzzes. Checking the screen, I see it's the caterer. As I talk with them about last-minute details, I watch Lizzy scoop up velvety brie with her cracker. Her hair is down right now, but she will put it up before the night's over. Lizzy has a wild mass of curly, dark brown hair. With today's humidity, it is especially unruly.

I nod in agreement with the caterer. "Yes, that's perfect."

Lizzy slides another cracker through the cheese. As I watch her, I decide her dress is flattering after all. Despite the yellow and orange, the dress is becoming on her and fits her body as if it were tailor-made.

"Yes, thank you so much. See you soon." I hang up with the caterers and chat with Lizzy about her new dress, before we hear Jake coming down the stairs. We are both in full entertainment mode now.

I watch him kiss Lizzy; she smiles, but the repulsion on her face is unmistakable. She isn't nearly as good at hiding her emotions as I am. By some miracle, Jake's charms have failed to work on Lizzy.

Jake is rambling on and on about golf. I make myself one cracker, tallying the calories in my head, and try to seem interested in what my husband is saying. I'm antsy to get this party going.

As if on cue, the side gate chirps. That will be the caterers. *Thank goodness!* Jake goes to let them in as the front door rings. *Here we go!* I pull open the door. Collin is standing there with his crooked smile and his heart on his sleeve. Beth is by his side, where she belongs, and I give them the usual air kiss and greet. We still have a while before anyone else is due to arrive, but Collin and Beth are family to me. Of course, they don't need an excuse to be early, although I hear Beth offering one.

I met Beth during my senior year of college. I always knew there would come a time when I would find a man who filled my needs. And when that time came, I wanted to have the perfect girl in place for Collin. Beth and I would go out for lunch, study at the library, and spend hours watching sappy movies together. I pretended to like them. I had to. This woman was essential to Collin's future.

I never took her to the apartment I shared with Collin. They would meet when I was ready, not a moment before. I know that sounds controlling or manipulative, but you have to understand, Collin never showed interest in anyone but me. I knew the timing would be crucial. When I met Jake, I knew that time had come.

Beth is everything I wish I could be: compassionate, honest, authentic. Most of all, *normal.* She is the kind of woman Collin deserves, regardless of his feelings for me. He doesn't understand it, but I only want what's best for him. He's been through so much with me, but I can't give him the relationship he has always wanted. All of my sharp edges would cut him to pieces, and I've done enough damage to Collin already.

The truth is, I never wanted a sensitive man who was in touch with his emotions. I didn't want to be gently loved and lightly caressed. I needed something else—a strong alpha male, the leader of the pack. I didn't want to be wooed. I wanted to be taken. I wanted a man who would take charge, lay down the law, and even be a tad barbaric. *Me Man, You Woman.* I found those things in Jake.

That being said, my sincere advice to you is to be careful what you wish for.

The caterers burst into the kitchen, accompanied by Jake, arms full of bins. I suggest we all go outside while they get things ready. I grab my bottle of wine and see Lizzy follow suit with hers. We all settle in together on the outdoor sectional. I notice my bracelet sparkling in the sun. I may have used Jake's money to buy it, but make no mistake, I'm the one who truly paid.

In the background, I hear Jake asking Collin about work.

"So Collin, how's work going, buddy?" Jake throws his arm

over me as he says it. *Me Man, You Woman.*

Collin *hates* when Jake calls him buddy, and Jake does it for no other reason than to piss him off. Beth swoops in to save him, redirecting Jake with nonsense about the barstools. *See?* This is why I chose her.

All of us, including Jake and Beth, can see how Collin looks at me with his lovesick puppy-dog eyes. It's not because he doesn't love Beth. Collin *does* love her, but he loves me too.

I try my best to neutralize it when Beth is around. But I need Collin in my life; he is my keel, keeping me upright. He has seen all of my ugly bits, and he loves me anyway. Everyone should have someone like Collin in their life. Only a lucky few have it, and the truth is, I'm the last one who deserves it.

It might help you understand my relationship with Collin if you think of us as twins. Picture the pair of us floating around in utero, sharing the same oxygen and blood. Me taking the lion's share of both, leaving him starving for nourishment. There's a word for that. It's called a parasitic twin. That's what I am—a parasite, sucking the life out of Collin and taking whatever I need.

I let out an audible sigh for things that never change and realize that Collin is watching me. I look at Beth and see that she is watching us both. If I was a better person, I would let Collin go.

I leave to speak to the caterers before we all trek back inside. The spread of food is impressive, covering most of our large kitchen island. There is enough here to feed a small army. My eyes race to scan Jake's face, and to my relief, he seems pleased. *Thank God.* Lizzy goes straight in, nabbing two of the crab croquettes for herself. My heart feels a little ping. *I really do love her.*

While Lizzy occupies herself with the food, I pull Beth to the side, trying to smooth any ruffled feathers. *I stumble out of the gate.* "Beth, you look fantastic." *I know. It sounds thin and weak. Let me try again,* "Those shoes are darling! Where did you get them?" *Yes, still terrible.* What am I supposed to say? "I'm so sorry your husband is in love with me, but you have nothing to worry about." *Yeah right! She needs a distraction. Here we go.* "I'm afraid Jake is having another affair." I try to squeak out a tear and barely manage a distressed expression, but this has her attention.

"Oh my God, Kimber, I'm so sorry."

She is genuinely upset. *Bless her heart.*

"Do you know who she is?"

I sigh and put my hand over my chest. In a whisper, I say, "I have no idea, but I'm sure of it." Beth looks absolutely wrecked for me.

Part of me wants to tell her the truth. Jake is always having an affair. It's the way our chaotic, tumultuous, sham of a relationship works. Despite that, he will never leave me, and I will never leave him. I don't understand the reasons behind that, but it is what it is. Jake and Kimber, till death do us part.

In any case, this seems to get Beth over the hump. "It feels so good to get that off my chest, Beth. Thanks."

"I'm here for whatever you need." She embraces me and pats my back in a hang-in-there sort of way.

The hug lasts a moment longer than I'm comfortable with, and I pull back. "I know you are, and that means so much to me."

It really does. "We should get back to the others, though." As the words come out of my mouth, I hear the doorbell ring.

We have more guests! In a sing-song voice, I chime, "Coming," and hurry to greet our much-anticipated cortege. Let the show begin.

CHAPTER EIGHT

Lizzy: Part One
Day of the Murder

I let myself into the Carter house through the stately red front door. I have always admired their grand entrance—the big chandelier winking at me from above, the marble floors, the sweeping staircase, and a regal round table resting in the center as a pulpit for ever-fresh flowers.

"Hello," I call out, my voice searching for an ear to connect with, even though I already know Kimber will be in the kitchen.

"Back here, Lizzy."

I find my friend, as expected, with a glass of wine tipped to her mouth—not an unfamiliar sight. Kimber smiles at me mid-swig and motions toward the kitchen counter. More than a dozen bottles of wine and a generous selection of hard liquors stand ready.

"Choose your poison." Kimber does a Vanna White sweep of her hand towards the assortment. After careful consideration, I settle on one of my favorite merlots. Wine is reasonably safe.

I give myself an ample pour. "I thought you might need help setting up," I say, swirling the wine around in my glass. I take a long, slow sip, letting the wine linger and spread throughout my mouth before swallowing. The flavor is rich and full. It's perfect and exactly what I need.

Kimber pats the back of her head, searching for rogue hairs that might have escaped her oh-so-perfect French twist. I don't think she realizes how often she does that in one evening, as though a misplaced hair would end the world. But that's Kimber. She's a perfectionist.

"There isn't anything to do." Kimber says. "Maria left a few minutes ago, and I'm having the party catered, just small plates." I watch her tip her glass again.

"Did Jake's soccer friends RSVP?" Kimber nods. "Yes, five couples are coming. I haven't met any of them before, but it will be nice to see some new people."

If there weren't so many guests tonight, we would have a formal, five-course dinner at the dining table. I'm not complaining, mind you, about the caterers. Their crab cakes have huge lumps of crab meat drizzled with a rich, creamy rémoulade. I can hardly wait.

Kimber giggles, "You're thinking of the crab croquettes, aren't you?"

Am I that transparent? "You can't blame me. You know how much I love them!"

"You have nothing to worry about. There will be plenty. I've ordered more than twice the usual amount. Kimber dries a knife and slides it back into the block. "But the food won't be here for a bit. Let me see what I can round up for a little snack."

She glances back in my direction with a smirk, "We know you don't do well drinking on an empty stomach."

I cringe at the memory. Last Fourth of July, I tossed my cookies all over Kimber's beautiful patio. At least I made it out of the pool. *That's something.* I shudder at the image of my partially digested hotdog chunks bobbing alongside the pool noodles. *Fricking tequila shots.* "I'm never living that down, am I?" I ask, taking my seat at the kitchen island.

As Kimber roots around in her enormous refrigerator, I can't help but appreciate how great her butt looks. It's as perky as ever. *Annoying.* Her firm tuchus puts my sad and tired set of pancakes to shame. How is that fair? Kimber doesn't even work out! I take another healthy sip of wine to soothe myself. *Maybe wine is not so safe after all.*

Kimber surfaces from the deep dive and sets the items on the counter. Brie, a jar of quince, and some prosciutto. *So Kimber.* If we were at my house, I would offer squirty cheese in a can and some stale crackers.

As I watch Kimber refill her glass, a diamond bracelet sings to me from her wrist. "Oh, my God! Is that new?" I grab her hand and pull it towards me. "It is gorgeous!"

She runs her finger over it. "It is. It came today."

"I *love* it. It's from Tiffany, isn't it?" She nods. I'm curious if Jake keeps track of how many shiny trinkets Kimber buys. It seems like she's been buying them more often lately. "Does Jake know?" I ask, poking my nose only a little bit into her business.

"I'm not sure," she answers with a smile.

Kimber takes a small paring knife out of the drawer and cuts the rind off the cheese. A little more wine slides down my throat

—the alcohol already purring in my brain.

"It's so much better baked," Kimber says, referring to the brie, "but in a pinch, I pop it in the microwave. It's still good." Kimber pushes some buttons on the microwave and grabs some crackers from the cabinet. "So, what's going on with you? How's Chloe?" She asks and adds, "I saw her swimming earlier."

I frown. "Oh, Chloe is fine. Normal teenage stuff. She thinks she is in love and has been floating around the house for months." I snort. "You know how it is."

"I do." She commiserates. "Have you met this young man yet?"

"I have." I puff air through my lips. "He's all wrong for her, but college starts in the fall, and there will be plenty of boys on campus to choose from. This guy is a total loser, but she can't see that through her rose-colored glasses." I take another sip from my nearly empty glass. "I have a feeling it will be over soon, so I'm not going to stress about it." I change the subject. "So, how are things going with the fundraiser at the hospital?"

Kimber beams. "Really well, I'm so glad you asked."

"Will you be able to donate?"

I wasn't planning on it. I curse myself for bringing it up.

Kimber reaches across the brie, touches my hand, and lowers her voice so the other nonexistent people in the room won't hear. "I know things aren't great with John's work. But no contribution is too small." *She should have been a politician.*

"Oh, things aren't that bad. I'll be happy to donate. Just remind me." It's not like John and I are hurting financially, but we aren't in the same league as the Carters—not even close! The amount of money they pay for parties alone is a small fortune.

"I'm so sorry John couldn't make it. Where is he off to this time?"

Lord knows. "I know this is awful, but I don't even ask anymore." I dig my cracker into the brie. "He's gone so much of the time. I've gotten used to flying solo." It's the truth, and I might even prefer it. Of course, I'm sure I'll miss him more once Chloe leaves for college. My heart feels a pang. *Empty nest. Home alone. No longer needed.* The thought sends a shiver down my spine.

Kimber opens her mouth to say something, but her cell phone rings.

Listening to Kimber's side of the conversation leads me to believe tonight's caterer is on the other end of the phone. I drag my cracker through my brie again and let my eyes wander. It's a beautiful house. You'd think I'd be most impressed with the ample space. It is grand, but what I envy the most is how clean and fresh it is. It's always as if they moved in yesterday with brand-new furniture. The vibe is light and airy. There's not a dusty surface in the whole place.

While Kimber is on her phone, I pull out mine and go straight to the Tiffany website. I search the gold inventory. My mouth drops. *Seven thousand dollars? Lord, have mercy!* I don't know why I'm surprised. It seems she always has a shiny new bobble.

Kimber, now done with her call, turns back to me with a big inhale and a cemented smile. "I love your dress, Lizzy." She says it with outlandish enthusiasm.

Ah. *There she is.*

Kimber has flipped a switch and turned on her *hostess*

mode. The transformation must have happened during her conversation with the caterers. They are two different people. Every day Kimber, who is my friend, and hostess Kimber, who is everyone's *way-too-happy* friend. I'm a little bit sad that hostess Kimber has shown up so soon.

She asks again, "Your dress—is it new? I haven't seen it before." She drains her glass and pours another.

My eyes drop to my dress as if I have to remind myself what I'm wearing. But of course, I know. I bought it specifically for tonight. The dress is a colorful, sixties-inspired sheath style with pockets. "It *is* new. I thought it felt very ...." I search for a word and land on *hipster.* I add, "I bought it at the new boutique in Franklin, Abbey's Closet, the one I told you about."

"It suits you!" Hostess Kimber says as she holds out her glass to connect with mine. We clink our glasses together in what I can only guess is a toast to my newfound hipsterness.

Toasting is something Kimber loves to do when she drinks, which is basically all the time. She will raise her glass to pretty much anything. And the more she drinks, the more frequent the toasts.

Last summer, Kimber binge-watched The Tudors. She shouted "HUZZAH" and clinked glasses at every opportunity. I was relieved when that played itself out, even though I will admit it was fun in the beginning.

A familiar noise rolls into the kitchen. Kimber and I exchange glances. We hear Jake before we see him as he trots down the back stairs, his dress shoes connecting with the wooden treads. "Ladies," he booms with arms open wide, flashing his movie-star smile. "How are the two prettiest girls in the neighborhood?" He greets me with a kiss too close to my mouth and moves on to his wife. She gets a kiss on the forehead. "You look beautiful, darling." Kimber flutters her eyelashes like Scarlet O'Hara.

Jake takes a glass and drops three ice cubes inside before adding gin and tonic water. After plunking in two lime wedges, he begins a diatribe about the book he is currently reading. According to Jake, the author missed the point of their own book. That is classic Jake, always knowing better than everyone else.

When that subject runs its course, he pivots to how he has upped his golf game. Included with his commentary is a complete demonstration of his pro technique. Kimber and I nod, waiting for a break in Jake's solo performance. Kimber glances at me, and I roll my eyes. The corner of her mouth turns up as she fights back a giggle.

Jake is still going strong when, thankfully, the motion sensor on the side of the house chirps. *Saved by the chirp. Huzzah!* I lift my glass to myself and take another sip of wine.

"Oh, that must be the caterers." Kimber directs this at Jake.

Before Jake is even out the back door, the bell rings at the front.Kimber sails to the foyer. *Dat da da daaaaa. Introducing Kimber, the fantastical mistress of ceremonies, lady of the house, and ringmaster for the evening. The crowd goes wild.*

Collin and Beth are the first guests to arrive. I can't see them from here, but I know that Kimber will greet them with a flurry of air kisses and compliments on their attire.

Collin is tall and lean. I eye him as he lopes in behind his wife. He goes straight for the liquor and pours out three fingers of bourbon.

"Hey, Lizzy, how's it going?" He knocks the glass back and pitches me a Cheshire cat grin. Beth waves. The three of us exchange pleasantries.

They are a handsome couple, and I love them both. Collin has chiseled features and a strong jaw. He is always a bit tatty—like he is right on the cusp of needing a haircut and a fresh shave. But not in an unattractive way, in a Marlboro man sort of way. Rugged and manly. His hair is forever tumbling down over his deep brown eyes. It's very sexy.

I'm afraid my husband, John, is average at best. He's put on about thirty pounds since we married, and now he's balding. The last time he was home, I noticed more hair growing out of his ears than on his head. In fairness, though, I'm no Miss America. It's been years since a man paid me any extra attention. Feeling a little sorry for the pair of us, I take another sip in consolation.

Beth looks over the selection and chooses a pinot noir. She is a wisp of a thing. I doubt she weighs a hundred pounds soaking wet with her boots on. Her hair is strawberry blonde, and she has an adorable smattering of freckles across the bridge of her nose. "Sorry, we're early." Beth gestures toward Collin. "My handsome husband over here wanted to make sure we got a spot in the driveway instead of parking on the street," Collin smirks, winking at her through his hair.

I pipe up. "That's true about most men. Isn"t it? They are always so concerned about how and where they park. John always backs into a spot. It's like we might need to make a quick getaway or something!"

Beth agrees and adds, "And they always zip right in. I worry about every inch when I'm backing up. Even when the reverse camera shows nothing behind me, I don't trust it."

Kimber is commiserating with Beth about the perils of parallel parking when the door flies open. Two plump women plunge into the kitchen, followed by Jake. Each with a plastic tote in their arms.

All three unload their bins onto the island. I watch as they put their hot pink aprons on, their name and logo proudly displayed on the front. A Cow Jumped over the Spoon Catering Company. The logo, as you can imagine, is a cow over a spoon. I can hardly wait to dig in.

"Everyone," Kimber says, like a headmistress addressing her class. "Let's go to the patio and let these lovely ladies do their job." As we all proceed outside, I see Kimber grab the bottle of wine she's been pulling from, a top-shelf pinot noir. I take my Merlot. I wouldn't want to get parched.

The mugginess this evening is unfortunate. It's unusual for this time of the year. Sometimes the parties work their way outside, but I doubt it will happen tonight.

I search my pocket for a hair tie and try to corral my hair into something acceptable. We all sink into the luxe outdoor furniture with a combined satisfied groan.

"So, Collin," Jake says as he puts a possessive arm over Kimber, "how's work going, buddy?"

Collin is clearly irritated by the question, but Jake pretends he's oblivious. Collin pushes the hair out of his face and replies, "Good. Things are good." His words hang in the air in an awkward moment of silence. We know that Collin doesn't like

Jake, including Jake. But he always acts like they're best friends to piss Collin off.

Beth comes to Collin's rescue. "Jake, are those new bar stools?"

Jake puffs up, proud of his outdoor bar, unaware of Beth's motive for asking. We all turn our heads, and indeed, six new stools cozy up to the sleek concrete counter. "Good eye for details, Beth," Jake replied, "the old ones had seen better days. I pitched them before the winter. I had these custom-made to go with the bar."

The conversation shifts to something else, and I zone out a bit. Light music floats out of speakers disguised as rocks. The sun is low in the sky. In a short time, the patio will be illuminated with a dozen lights nestled throughout the landscaping. I watch a dragonfly skim across the cool blue water of the pool. It all seems so idyllic. So perfect. *Too perfect.*

I refill my glass and force myself to tune in to the conversations around me. "... And just like that!" Jake is still talking, as usual. "I'm not kidding! That's exactly how it happened. The rest is history!" I have no idea what he's talking about, and I don't care. Jake never says anything of substance.

Turning to Beth, I open my own conversation. "So, Beth, tell me how your remodel is going. I only hear bits and pieces from Kimber."

"It' should be over soon. Thank God." She raises both hands in a hallelujah kind of way. "It's so awkward to share your house with strangers coming and going all day. I tried to talk Collin into going on a cruise while the work was ongoing, but he doesn't trust leaving our house to them. So, I was designated by my wonderful husband as—project overseer, my official title. I have a badge and everything!" Beth laughs at her joke and turns to her husband, but Collin's eyes are fixed on Kimber. He hasn't heard a word she's said. Beth turns back to me and manages a smile with a shrug.

After more light conversation, the caterers come out and wave at Kimber. "It's all set. We'll come by tomorrow to pick up the plates." Kimber stands and goes to talk to them. I can't hear what they're saying. But the conversation ends with crisp hugs and fake kisses. Kimber motions toward us and asks, "Is anyone hungry?"

We all file back in and ooh and aah over the food. It's a self-serve concept; each delicious creation is presented on a tiny square plate. I want one of everything, but the crab is calling my name. I snag a delicious croquette and then a second. If you ask me, they should give you two per plate to begin with.

Kimber and Beth have moved into the living room. Their voices are low. A little girl-talk, I guess. I am parked back on my stool, and the men are across from me talking. *Oof. Poor Collin.*

Jake is rattling on about *cleaning up* on yet another investment deal, his self-admiration in full swing. And as much as I don't like him, I have to admit that Jake is a good-looking man, like a *really* good-looking man. As he gestures, I can see his muscles move beneath his shirt. Physically, I would say Jake is the perfect male specimen.

Collin looks like he is about to boil over, clenching and unclenching his jaw, his hand balled into a fist on the counter. A vein in his neck is notably pulsing. His blood pressure must be through the roof right now.

He needs saving. *Lizzy to the rescue.* "Collin, Kimber told me you play the guitar." I cluck my tongue, "After all these years, I can't believe I didn't know that."

Collin turns toward me with an expression of relief. "Aw, I don't play too much anymore. It was something I picked up in high school. Beth still asks me to play her something every once in a while."

With Jake still standing there, I need to keep going. "Well, I've always admired people who could play an instrument. When I was in middle school, my best friend wanted to join the orchestra. So, of course, I did too. She picked the cello, and I picked the viola." I shake my head. "Don't ask me why. I mean, who chooses the viola?" I point at myself with both thumbs. "This girl, that's who!" I snort. "Anyway, I was so terrible that after three weeks of practicing, my mother bribed me to quit."

"You're joking." Collin laughs.

"No. I'm dead serious. She said if I would give up the viola, she would buy me a new bike with all the bells and whistles. Needless to say, I took the bike. And that was the end of my musical pursuit."

Bored, Jake finally moves on. Collin winks at me and says, "Thanks, Lizzy. I owe you one!"

CHAPTER NINE

Julian

Two Weeks & Two Days Before the Murder

The waitress asks me if I would like another drink. My answer, of course, is "Yes, please." I have a meeting with the PI I hired. My wife, Susan, is cheating on me. I can feel it. Did she think I wouldn't? We've been married for eleven years—the best eleven years of my life. I would be lost without her.

I pull out my phone, check my emails, and do today's Wordle. I'm trying to busy myself. The private investigator is late, and I'm uncomfortable sitting here alone. It gives me anxiety. In truth, everything gives me anxiety. I'm working on it in therapy, but my progress is slow. A stone sits in my stomach as I wait to hear what Susan has done.

It's a weird feeling—waiting for bad news. Part of you wants it to come quickly, so the dread of hearing whatever it is will be over. But the other part wants to hang on to the life you have now—the life before learning the truth about the horrible thing that has happened. *And I do know something horrible has happened.* I'm sure of it.

The man I hired passes by the restaurant's front window and enters through the door. He's a toad of a man with a croaky voice and bulging eyes. I give a little wave. *Here I am. Come ruin my life.* The man slides into his side of the booth. "Sorry, I'm late. The traffic was terrible."

"Oh, no worries." *Ha! No worries.* What a joke. I take a full swig of my bourbon and ginger and brace myself.

The investigator lifts the flap on his bag and pulls out a manilla folder. "So, I'll get right to it. Your wife is having an affair. She has been seeing a man named Jake Carter."

I take another healthy sip.

"They hook up every Tuesday and Thursday around lunchtime. I have pictures."

Oh, God. Pictures? Hard swallow. "Okay."

The investigator lays out the photos in front of me. I see a very muscular man and my wife through our bedroom window. They are in various intimate poses." *Our house?* Why would she take him to our house? "Who is this guy?"

"He is a high-profile attorney. You might have seen him on billboards around town." He gathers up the pictures and puts them back in the folder. "I'm sorry; I know how hard this is. I've been there. It's one thing to suspect an affair, and a whole other thing to see the proof."

I close my eyes and rub my forehead. I can get through this. "Can you tell me anything else about him?"

The investigator takes out his reading glasses and refers to his notes. "Yeah. He's married. Two kids. He goes to the gym every morning. I think that's where he met your wife." He looks up at me. "I tailed him for a few weeks. I know that your wife isn't his only sidepiece."

"Sidepiece? Please don't refer to my wife as that. Shit." I swallow the last of my bourbon and hold up my finger. The waitress nods.

"I was just trying to convey that I don't think it's any sort of love affair. All they do is meet and have sex. He leaves as soon as he ... when it's over. If that makes you feel any better."

"It doesn't."

"Right. Sorry. Let's see ... He is on a men's soccer team. It's an over-forties team in a rec league. The Brentwood Bombers. If you want to see him in person, you can find him here." He slides a piece of paper with an address and a map across the table. "They practice Monday and Wednesday at 6:00 p.m. on this field." He circles the location with his pen.

"I'm sorry to be the bearer of bad news, but that's the job. Never once have I been hired to find out if a partner is cheating, and they haven't been. Where there's smoke, there's fire. You know what I'm saying?"

I nod. "Well, thanks, I guess."

The man scoots out of the bench and leaves me the folder full of photos I never want to see again and a map. I put my head in my hands. *Shit.* Now that I know the truth, what do I do about it?

Today is Wednesday. I guess I'll see if I can join a soccer team.

CHAPTER TEN

Collin: Part One
MNPD Criminal Investigations Division
Homicide Unit

Oh my God! I cannot believe my good fortune! I've been racking my brain for the last four days trying to figure out a way to kill that son of a bitch without landing in jail, and someone else has beat me to it! Unbelievable!

Make no mistake; I was steadfast in my decision to kill Jake. I would make sure he would never hit Kimber again. But I wasn't about to do it in a house full of people. My thought was to lure him out to the middle of nowhere and end him there. Hopefully, finding a way to dispose of his body so it would never be found.

When I left Kimber the other day, I knew she was lying. Did she think I bought that load of crap she was trying to sell me? There's no way she asked Jake to beat her like that. That's ridiculous!

I only pretended to believe her so I would have time to devise a plan. But the Lord works in mysterious ways. Jake is dead, and I don't have to go to prison. *Hallelujah.*

So, who was it? That's the million-dollar question, right? I've been going over the night in my mind. There must be a clue somewhere.

Beth and I arrived early. Kimber was doing her hostess with the mostess schtick. Of course, Jake was his usual dickhead self. We got drinks and sat outside for a while. Not long after that, other guests began to arrive. Everyone was talking and laughing.

It felt like every other party. And then the next thing I knew—BAM—it was as if a bomb had exploded in the foyer. The sound coming from Kimber scared the crap out of me. It didn't even sound human. I thought I had heard every scream, cry, and wail that Kimber could produce, but I was wrong. Something happened to Kimber when she saw Jake's body. She broke.

I found her standing in the foyer with both hands pressed over her mouth, looking down at her dead husband. She looked so small standing beside Jake's fractured body. Somehow, even in death, Jake was still able to diminish her.

I only had a split second with Kimber before handing her over to Beth. After that, things moved at lightning speed. The cops loaded the lot of us into the backseats of patrol cars for transport here. Husbands and wives could ride together, but we were asked not to talk about what happened or use cell phones—with a friendly reminder that police vehicles are equipped with recording devices. Beth cried the entire drive.

So here we are, waiting our turn to be questioned. Beth's head rests on my shoulder. The weight of it tells me she has given herself over to sleep. I hope she has found peace there without fragments of what she saw tonight invading her dreams.

Across the room, Allie rests on several chairs. Her pregnancy belly button pushing against the delicate fabric of her dress. My eyes shift from Allie to her husband. A search of Eli's face tells me nothing. No one would blame Eli if he isn't too broken up about what happened tonight.

Over the years, I've watched Jake cut his brother off at the knees every chance he got. No matter what successes Eli had, Jake was quick to point out how insignificant they were compared to his own. It pissed me off to no end, but Eli is a sensitive guy, and Jake was his brother. Maybe for Eli, that counts for something.

The door pushes open, and a man calls Eli's name. Eli immediately looks at his sleeping wife. I can tell he doesn't want to leave her. He catches my eye. I give him the chin up, meaning I got this, and I watch as the two men vanish behind the door.

My mind circles back to the reason we are all here. Someone put a knife through Jake's heart. I scroll through the guests at the party in my head. If I've counted right, twenty-one of us were at the party, including our hosts. Jake didn't kill himself. *Twenty.* Kimber is a great actress, but there's no way she faked that. So, Kimber's out, and you already know it wasn't me. That leaves *eighteen* suspects. Eli doesn't have it in him to kill his brother or anyone else. *Seventeen.* A woman didn't do this. *Seven.*

We are left with the young husband of that office aide, Jake's partner Thomas, and the five soccer guys. Thomas has the body and balls of an accountant. *Sorry, accountants*, but you know what I mean, and the kid was pretty skinny. It's unlikely either one of them could get the jump on Jake.

My money is on one of the soccer guys. I bet Jake pissed one of them off with his bragging and bravado. If not that, it's possible Jake was sleeping with one of their wives. That wouldn't surprise me. *Shit*, it wouldn't surprise me if I found out he screwed *all* their wives.

I am beyond pumped that someone else did the deed. Bravo, to whoever it was. Even if a tiny part of me feels a little disappointed that I didn't get the satisfaction of doing it myself. But it's hard to get away with murder nowadays. There are cameras everywhere. GPS is in our cell phones and in our cars, not to mention the advances in touch DNA. So, I'm going to take this as a win.

I bet you have some questions for me. You're curious about my relationship with Kimber and my feelings for her. So let's get it out of the way. Yes, I am in love with Kimber. I have always been in love with her, and I always will be. Nothing will ever change that.

We met on the first day of ninth grade. Kimber walked into our high school with her ponytail swinging side to side, wearing a short denim skirt and a white Izod polo. A pink notebook was crooked on her right arm. I'll never forget the way the morning sun illuminated her slight silhouette. She looked like an angel sent to Earth just for me. It was love at first sight.

The rest of the morning, I searched the halls for that perfect blonde ponytail in a sea of bobbing heads. I had to talk to this girl. She already had my heart in her hand, and we hadn't even exchanged a word.

I had my hopes pinned on lunch. With any luck, that's where

I would find her. I remember watching the clock, listening to my biology teacher drone on and on, waiting on the lunch bell. When it finally rang, I vaulted out of my chair, praying that this girl and I shared the same lunch period.

The lunch room was chaotic, being the first day of school. Everyone was trying to claim a table for their clique. I did a quick scan of the room and didn't see her. It knocked the wind out of my sails. For a second, I wondered if the whole thing was a dream. But then, there she was. A living, breathing, actual girl.

She was sitting alone in the back of the room, carefully unwrapping a granola bar. I strode to her table with my best swag, sat opposite her, and introduced myself. *Bold for a ninth-grader, I know, but I was a confident kid.*

We connected right away and spent the whole lunch talking. Kimber explained that her family moved to the area from Michigan over the summer. She was happy about that because she hated the snow and cold weather. Her dad was a big-shot CEO for an inventory management company. He traveled a lot, and most of the time, her mother joined him.

Her full name was Kimber Johanna Hilliard. The Johanna part came from her grandmother. A spitfire who hula danced for soldiers during World War II. Kimber went on to say that she was an only child and that she was a mistake. Her parents never intended to have children. All the words bubbled out of her as if she had been waiting a very long time for someone to talk to.

Then Kimber asked about me and listened to everything I had to say. This gorgeous girl seemed into me and even suggested meeting up after school. It felt like I had won the lottery! Even though, at the time, I had no idea what I was getting myself into. Sometimes I wonder if I would choose to sit across from her again if I knew how it would all turn out. I'm not sure that I would.

Regardless, I spent the rest of that day sailing around the school in an infatuation stupor. Riding the waves of the good life—my new life with Kimber. Images of us kissing in the park, holding hands through the halls, and spending afternoons wrapped in each other's arms rippled through my mind. My enthusiasm for our budding relationship was off the charts. I even wrote *Kimber Montgomery* inside my algebra folder to see what it looked like. I remember thinking it looked pretty damn spectacular.

There was something magical about the way Kimber made me feel—a skip in my heart, a weird little flutter. I knew it was a once-in-a-lifetime thing, even at that age. Whatever you want to call it, I still experience it every time I see her. *Every single time.*

Sadly, when we met later that afternoon, Kimber planted me squarely in the friend zone. She told me, in no uncertain terms, that she wanted a best friend, not a boyfriend. Period.

Sure, it was a bummer, but I was willing to accept her conditions. I wanted to be with her, whatever that meant. She would come around. I was positive that I'd be able to win her over one day. *Remember, I thought I had game.* Unfortunately, that didn't pan out, and I've been languishing on the sidelines of Kimber's life ever since.

We quickly became inseparable, and within weeks, Kimber was the most important person in my life. She became a need, a requirement for life—air. Whatever seeds Kimber planted in my heart that day took root. And have since traveled through every vein, artery, and bone. She became as much a part of me as I am myself.

We were only fourteen that day in the lunchroom. As it turned out, we were born only hours apart. We compared birth certificates and found that Kimber is older by two hours and fifty-six minutes.

Our situation was unusual. Kimber's parents were wrapped up in their own lives. They were gone all the time, traveling the world, busy with one social function after another. They left her alone to fend for herself. I guess they figured at that age, she was grown enough. So, they let her make her own decisions and come and go as she pleased. They put money in an account monthly to pay for food, taxis, supplies, and whatever else she might need. As long as her grades were decent, they stayed off her back.

My parents were unusual, too. They were extraordinarily liberal—modern hippies, free love, and all of that. So, by that first summer, Kimber lived with me full-time. We slept in my room, in my bed, with the door closed. She slept in panties alone, and I slept in boxers.

Kimber had rules. She allowed me to hold her, and she didn't care if I touched her boobs. So, I always fell asleep with her small breast in my hand. She rolled her eyes and said, "Collin, they're just boobs. I don't care if you touch them or not."

It was a long time before I could lie beside her without getting an erection. Finally, I learned that if I concentrated on syncing my breathing with hers, my body would relax. Allowing me to follow her into the vast fields of sleep, playing hide and seek with her in our dreams.

That trick worked in bed, but there was nothing I could do about it when we started taking showers together. My rock-hard penis was always there, front and center, without fail, but Kimber never commented on my erections. It didn't seem to phase her either way. After a while, we were together so much that my body stopped reacting, at least most of the time. That's not to say the desire wasn't there. Of course it was.

I think about those showers all the time. That's where I felt closest to Kimber. We had a routine. She washed my hair, and then I would wash hers. It was the same with our bodies. I loved how she felt under my soapy hands. And how she giggled every time I went under her arms. We cleaned our own genitals. That was another one of Kimber's rules. Sometimes, I would *clean* mine after she was out of the shower. I suspect she knew what I was really doing, but if she did, she never said anything about it.

One shower with her stands out in my mind. We were sixteen. Kimber hadn't started having periods yet. But, at the time, we didn't know that was unusual. Kimber didn't have any girlfriends to talk to about it. Her mother was absent from her life, and she didn't want to ask my mom about it. So, we had no idea when it would happen.

That moment came for her while she was in the shower with me. "Oh my God, Kimber, you're bleeding."

She looked down and put her hand between her legs. "Oh my gosh. Is this …." I could see the shock in her eyes. "I thought it would hurt, but I don't feel anything." She held up her bloody fingers. "Oh, gross!"

I had no idea how to react or what to do. "Do you want me to go get my mom?"

She was horrified. "Absolutely not! Jeez, Collin. You know how I am. This is private!"

"Well, what do we do then?"

"Go into your mom's bathroom and see if she has anything. I guess, like a pad or tampon. I'll stay here in the shower."

I wrapped a towel around my waist and poked my head out of our bathroom to see if the coast was clear. I could hear my mom in the kitchen singing Volare. She always sang that song when she was cooking spaghetti and meatballs. I knew she'd be busy stirring the sauce, so I tiptoed down the hall and snuck into my parents' bathroom.

I didn't know where to find them. So I started going through drawers. It was a little weird thinking about my mom having a period. She was my *mom*. Within that bubble, she wasn't a sexual person in any way, shape, or form.

Finally, I found a box of tampons under the sink. I kept looking for pads but never found any. Tampons would have to do. I took three out of the box.

Kimber was still standing in the shower when I returned, her hair wrapped in a towel. "Ok, I found these." I showed her the three tampons. "So, what now? You want me to leave?"

"No. Hang on." She held a washcloth between her legs while waddling to the toilet. She sat down and said, "Okay, give me one."

I watched her unwrap it. I guess she was testing it out, but she pushed the plunger too hard, forcing the cotton part of the tampon to shoot out of the other side and onto the floor. "Shoot!" She held out her hand. "Give me another one."

I handed Kimber another and watched as she spread her legs. "Umm, do you need any help?"

"I don't know. Maybe." She positioned the tip of the applicator against her, and pushed the plunger again. This time, the tampon fell into the toilet. "Ugh!"

I offer, "I think you have to put the first part inside you and *then* push the actual tampon through it."

Kimber took the towel off her head and threw it on the ground. "You know what? I'm going to get on the floor, and you're going to do it."

"I'm going to do it? I don't know, Kimber. What if it hurts you?"

"Collin! I'm not worried about that right now. Just get it in." Kimber moved from the toilet to the floor and closed her eyes. "Ok, I'm ready." She took a deep breath. "Do it!"

I knelt next to her and unwrapped the last tampon. "If this doesn't work, we should get my mom."

"It's going to work, Collin! Stop yapping and do it already!"

"You need to open your legs a little wider." She did. "Okay, I see ... the hole." I gently slid the applicator in about halfway. It wasn't hard at all. "Okay, I'm going to push it in now. There it goes."

"Did you do it?"

"I guess so." I pulled the applicator away. "I can see the string hanging out. I think that's right. Can you feel it?"

"Not at all." Kimber sat up. "How do I know when to change it?"

"I have no idea, but we'll need to get more." I left Kimber home and biked the two miles to Walgreens. To our relief, the box I bought had instructions inside. Together, Kimber and I read about the dangers of leaving the tampon in too long and studied the diagram of how to insert them. I was proud that I was successful with my first attempt.

I know all this sounds very abnormal to you, but somehow to us, it felt normal. I loved Kimber, and Kimber loved me. We were there for each other. Life was easy together, and we fell into a rhythm of synchronicity.

Everything changed when Kimber and I discovered the mind-bending effects of alcohol. Drinking was fun in the beginning. A few beers provided a nice little buzz, but we soon learned that liquor gave you more bang for the buck. I knew when to stop, but Kimber struggled.

By the time we turned seventeen, she was drinking daily, mostly vodka. It seemed as though she drank it by the gallon. I never understood how this petite, delicate girl could drink all day long and still be going into the night. I bet she could drink any man under the table.

My parents were oblivious. Kimber was an expert at hiding her drinking and its effects from everyone but me. And when she went off the rails, I was left to deal with the consequences. The alcohol took her to dark, ugly places. I suspected that something happened to her in the past, maybe when she was little, but she said I was being ridiculous. Regardless, the more she drank, the further down the rabbit hole she'd go, dragging me down with her. Kimber's drinking took a toll on both of us.

I tried to temper her where I could, but Kimber was volatile, sometimes turning on herself with whatever sharp thing was handy. The war she raged against her body terrified me. I was losing her. She was losing herself.

"Look, Collin," she said one day, "we need to talk about the fact that I'm going to start having sex. I know you're not going to like it, but it's going to happen."

"Have sex with who? You haven't even kissed anyone!" I was incredulous. "You've never been on a single date!" I could feel my blood rising.

"I don't have to be dating anyone, Collin." She paused, "It's not up for discussion. I just wanted to prepare you. There will be no defending my honor, no punches thrown, no temper tantrums. It is what it is, and you'll have to deal with it." Then she added, "If it makes you feel any better, I don't plan on kissing anyone. Ever."

And that was that. Arguing with Kimber about anything has always been futile. We would go round and round, but the outcome was always the same. "If you don't like it, Collin, I'll go back to my parents' house. I told you what our relationship boundaries were, and you agreed."

Of course, she was right. I did agree. Kimber never waivered on the rules and never led me to believe we would be anything more than what we were already, whatever that was.

Two weeks after that conversation, Kimber and I were at some random house party—our usual weekend activity. I watched as Kimber sidled up to a guy. I recognized him from another high school. He was a super jock and one of their star football players. Tom something. They talked for less than ten minutes before she led the way into a back room and shut the door.

It felt like a punch in the stomach. I tried *so* hard not to think about what this guy was doing to her, but that was impossible. Where are his hands? Is he inside? Does it hurt her? It was excruciating.

We drove home in silence, and when we got home, I asked her to shower with me. I needed that time with her, but it was all too much, and in the middle of washing her hair, I started crying. I couldn't help myself. Kimber turned and pulled me to her.

"I'm sorry, Collin. I'm so, so sorry. I'm not trying to hurt you. I swear I'm not."

I do believe she meant it. But, despite that, her disappearing with different guys became a regular thing. One night, after disappearing twice with two different guys, I had to confront her. My grief turned into anger.

"Kimber! I'm so sick of this shit. I hate that these assholes have their hands all over you. I don't understand. I'm right here. I love you. Why not me?"

"You're never going to get it, Collin. There's no use trying to explain it to you."

"Please, Kimber. Please try. I don't know what you see in those guys. They're all losers."

"It's not about the guys, Collin. It's *never* been about the guys," she said, rolling her eyes, annoyed with me already. "The sex with them *disgusts* me, and I hate myself for doing it. That's the whole point. It's a kind of punishment. It's a way to hurt myself without the cutting." Kimber traced the jagged white lines on her arm with her finger. "No scars for people to see."

"But that doesn't make any sense. Punished for what? What horrible thing have you done?"

She didn't have an answer.

I took her hand and begged, "Kimber, please let me make love to you. It would be different with me because I love you. I love you so much."

Kimber shook her head. "If we ever had sex, Collin, it would ruin everything we have together! You would be one of *them*, and I'd hate you with all my heart." She crossed her arms. "I love you the only way I can, Collin. Truly!" Kimber turned to leave the room, and as she was walking out the door, she said, "I knew you wouldn't understand. I'm not going to talk about it anymore."

So that became our new normal. Kimber would drink, do damage to herself, and then leave me with the aftermath.

Every time she acted out, whether it was the cutting or the random boys, she lost bits of herself. It fell on me to pick up whatever pieces were left and put Kimber back together.

A man comes through the door and calls Beth's name. There is no response, so I give her a nudge. She opens her eyes, but she still isn't one hundred percent with us.

It only takes a second before I can see on her face that she remembers where we are and why we are here. She rises and steadies herself, turning to me with a weak smile before disappearing down the hall.

CHAPTER ELEVEN

Beth Montgomery
MNPD Criminal Investigations Division
Homicide Unit

I hear my name. Is someone calling me? Where am I? Collin nudges me and says, "Beth, it's your turn."

"Hmmm? My turn for what?" I'm confused. "What's happening?"

He pushes the hair away from my eyes. "It's your turn to talk to the detective."

Oh. Yes. Jake is dead. It all comes rushing back. I saw him at the bottom of the stairs with a knife in his chest. I stand and walk toward the man at the door. My interview shouldn't take long. I don't know anything. And Lord knows I didn't want Jake dead, for so many reasons.

The detective leads me back to a small room with a table and two chairs. He indicates that I should take a seat. "Would you like some water? Coffee?"

I'm thirsty, but I don't want any delays. I only want to be home. "No, thank you. I'm fine."

"Okay." He settles in his seat and begins, "I'm sorry it's taken me so long to get to you. I will be as brief as possible."

"I appreciate that. I'm exhausted."

He gives me a reassuring nod, indicating that he indeed understands my exhaustion. And by the looks of him, I believe it.

"How long have you known the victim?"

"About twenty years. I met Kimber first, but it wasn't long before she started seeing Jake. Something like nine months before."

"Twenty years is a long time," he jots something in his book. "So, you are good friends."

"Yes, very."

The detective straightens out his leg and winces. "Forgive my unprofessional posture. I have a bad knee. The damp air is playing a number on it."

"It doesn't bother me a bit. Please sit however you're comfortable."

"Thank you." He gives me a weary smile. "Let me begin by asking if you noticed anything out of the ordinary tonight. Was there anything unusual that stands out in your mind?"

"No, nothing at all. It was like any other *Jake and Kimber* party. Good food. Good drinks. Small talk. A chance to dress up and get out of the house."

"So, you were drinking?"

"Yes, I was. But I wasn't driving."

"No, worries. I'm trying to get a feel for the atmosphere at the party." His demeanor is warm. "So, how many drinks did you have tonight?"

"I wasn't keeping track. Probably four glasses of wine. But we arrived earlier than the other guests."

"Okay. What time was that?"

"Around 6:30 or so."

He makes another note in his book. "What can you tell me about the Carter's marriage?"

I think back on my earlier conversation with Kimber. I don't want to betray her confidence, but this is a police investigation. "I know they had their problems." I shift in my seat. "Like everybody else does."

"Are you aware of any affairs?"

I have to tell him. "Kimber confided in me tonight that she suspected Jake was having an affair currently. And I also know of another one from some years ago.

"Did she tell you who the current affair was with?"

"No. Kimber said she had no idea." I'm uncomfortable talking about this. "To clarify, I don't know if she was one hundred percent sure about a current affair. I'm pretty sure she only *strongly* suspected."

He nods. "What do you know about the earlier affair? Do you know who that was with?"

"No, she never told me who, but I remember she was very upset about it. She caught them together in her own bed."

"What about affairs on her side? Does she have any boyfriends or love interests?"

"No. I'm not aware of any. And I'm confident Kimber would have told me if there had been anyone else."

"Okay," The detective pulls a prescription bottle out of his pocket and shakes out two pills. He throws them in his mouth, followed by a gulp of coffee. "Did you happen to see anyone go up the back stairs tonight?"

"No, I didn't notice anyone, but I wasn't paying attention to what everyone else was doing."

The detective refers to his notes. "Your husband's name is Collin. Is that correct?"

"Yes, that's right."

"You never saw him go upstairs?"

"No, I didn't." *Why is he asking that?*

Detective Parker tilts his neck to each side, producing a cracking sound. "Did your husband get along with Jake?"

No, Collin hated everything about him. "Yes, they got along fine. They socialized during the parties." My mouth is getting dry. I should have taken the water. "I mean, they didn't hang out or play golf or anything like that, but they were friendly. They have different interests." *Except for one.*

"They've never argued?"

"No." That's true. Collin was always on his best behavior with Jake. He would rather die than risk upsetting Kimber. *Now, I'm the one wincing from the pain.* My husband's love for Kimber is almost unbearable sometimes. "No," I say quietly, "they never argued."

"Did you see Jake and Thomas Martin arguing tonight?"

"No." *Thomas? I can't imagine him doing this.* "I've always found Thomas to be very soft-spoken."

"Did you notice Jake arguing with anyone else? His wife, maybe?"

"No, in fact, I saw the opposite. Jake came up, whispered in Kimber's ear, and kissed her forehead. I remember thinking how romantic it was that Jake took that moment to show her affection. It was sweet."

"So, despite her telling you that he could be having an affair, you think their marriage was in a good place?"

"Well, when you say it that way, it sounds silly. But *if* he was having an affair, it doesn't mean he couldn't still be in love with Kimber." *I know for a fact that one man can love two women.*

Parker chews on that for a minute. "Do you know of anyone that would want to harm Jake?"

Besides my husband? "No. I have no idea who would have done this. I don't know anything about Jake's teammates, though. Tonight was my first time seeing them. I have no idea what kind of people they are, but they all seemed pleasant enough. A few of them were a little rough around the edges."

"Where were you when Mrs. Carter discovered the body?"

"I was talking in the living room with my husband and Allie Carter."

"What about Eli Carter?"

"I remember Eli was in the living room with us until ten minutes or so before everything went nuts. He left to get a drink. I remember seeing him and Lizzy coming from the kitchen as we all ran to the foyer. The group of us got there at the same time. We were all standing together, and then Collin took charge."

"How did he take charge?"

I don't want to think about it. "Collin turned Kimber away from Jake's body." *He pulled her into him.* "He said someone needed to call 911." *I saw his body melt into hers.* "One of the soccer guys said he had already called." *He gave Kimber to me, and I saw the look on his face.* "After that, we all went to the living room to wait for the police to arrive."

"I see." Detective Parker pushes back his chair. "Is there anything else that might be helpful to the investigation?"

"No. I'm sorry."

He rises, offers me his hand and a business card. "Thank you for your time, Mrs. Montgomery."

I follow him back down the hall. He holds the door open for me and calls Collin. I catch Collin's eyes as we pass. It scares me to not know what he's thinking. Half the time, his mind is somewhere else. I should say it's with *someone* else. I take my seat and think about the last twenty years.

From the beginning, I thought Collin's relationship with Kimber was strange. They were too close—more than best friends. But Kimber had Jake, so I wasn't too worried about it.

When Collin and I got married, I expected things to change. But I was wrong about that. A part of his heart is inaccessible to me. That part belongs to Kimber. He loves her as much as he loves me, only in different ways.

Every night, Collin calls out Kimber's name while he's sleeping. I've never told him that he does it. I don't want him to know. He has no control over who he dreams about. My only consolation is that he doesn't say her name in a sexual, moaning way. It sounds more like she's lost and he's searching for her.

I never wake him up when he's dreaming. I decided a long time ago to let him keep looking for Kimber in the depths of his mind. If I allow Kimber to saturate his unconscious, the conscious Collin might be more present with me. It's the best I can hope for.

I spin my wedding ring around on my finger. I know Collin

loves me, but now that Jake's gone, I don't know if that's enough.

CHAPTER TWELVE

Collin Montgomery: Part 2
MNPD Criminal Investigations Division
Homicide Unit

I watch the door close behind Beth. My heart follows her down the hall. Beth deserves better. She deserves someone there for her one hundred percent of the time, and I will never be that person.

I know it's hard to understand my relationship with Kimber. We aren't just friends. We aren't brother and sister. We aren't lovers. Whatever you want to call it, we are tethered together forever through rage and grief, belonging and devotion, love and desperation. Kimber is in me, and I am in her. I can't change that any more than I can change the phases of the moon or the setting sun.

That doesn't mean I will ever leave Beth for Kimber. I would *never* do that. And not because Kimber doesn't want me as a husband, but because I love Beth. I made a promise to her on the day we married, and I will keep that promise forever. I have never kissed Kimber, and I never will.

I do remember the last time I tried, though. It was during our senior year of high school. We were in Florida for spring break. We'd been drinking since morning, but Kimber was in a great mood. She was running down the boardwalk, singing and dancing. "Collin, I can hear the water calling for me." She took off running. "C'mon, Collin! Let's go swimming!"

All the bars were closed, and the beach was empty. The possibility of sharks skittered through my mind. But without hesitation, Kimber peeled off her clothes and ran to the sea.

The moon was the thinnest of slivers that night, and Kimber disappeared into the glossy black water. Fear aside, I stripped off my clothes and went to her. She was farther out than I realized. The water rose to my chest before I reached her.

She swam to me through the temperate water, wrapping herself around me—arms around my neck, legs hitched around my waist, and my hands on her bare bottom, supporting her weight.

I knew better, but I tried to kiss her anyway. "No, Collin. Please don't ruin it. Let's just be like this, you and me. Surrender to the tug of the tide. Let yourself go, Collin. Feel the water breathe."

I closed my eyes and let myself sway with the water instead of trying to stand against it. Kimber was right. Each pull felt like a breath drawn. I gave myself over to the ebb and flow and the feeling of Kimber's flesh pressed against mine.

The sensation was intoxicating and the most intimate experience of my life. I can't even guess how long we stayed that way. Kimber clinging to me in the Gulf of Mexico, feeling the energy between us and the sea. I could have stayed there with her forever.

That night in Florida was two years before Kimber met Jake.

Kimber and I were living together in a two-bedroom apartment, even though we were still sleeping in the same room—the same bed.

It was the middle of the week, a Wednesday night. Kimber and I were at our favorite neighborhood bar, celebrating our twenty-second birthday. Kimber made a toast. "To us and our birthdays!" We clinked glasses and laughed. She was the most beautiful woman in the world that night.

The man on the stool next to Kimber overheard her toast and offered to buy her a drink. She replied, "Only if you buy my friend one too."

He shot me a look and grinned. "I'll do better than that!" He stood up and spoke to the room. "Everyone can have a round on me in celebration of this ravishing woman's birthday!"

There were cheers and happy birthdays around the bar. Jake, the victor, took the spoils. He spent the rest of the night monopolizing Kimber's attention. She was enamored. He was an up-and-coming lawyer, landing a job at one of the most respected law firms in town right out of college.

After that night, Jake was a fixture in our lives. It was clear that he was different from the other guys. He was the only man Kimber slept with more than once. I knew that was a big deal for her. She seemed happy, even grounded. As unbearable as it was, I stood aside and watched the love of my life seemingly fall in love with someone who wasn't me.

About a month into her relationship with Jake, Kimber introduced me to Beth. The four of us went on endless double dates together. Of course, I realized Kimber was trying to set me up, but I didn't mind. The double dates allowed me to keep watch over Kimber. When she needed me, I wanted to be there for her.

I looked for clues—some sign that Kimber was struggling. I was waiting for her to fall apart so I could put her back together, like always. But that never happened. She didn't need me anymore. She had Jake. Kimber's relationship with him tempered her. She was in a good mood all the time. It was time for me to face the facts. Jake was giving her something I couldn't. I had to let her go.

Defeated, I turned to Beth. She was attractive, wholesome, level-headed, and worlds away from Kimber. Our relationship was easy and uncomplicated, and the biggest thing—she wanted me. With Beth, I didn't fall in love. I made the decision to walk into it.

We married a few months after Kimber married Jake. I accepted the situation for what it was and built a life with Beth. We bought a house, adopted a dog, and before long, both Beth and Kimber were pregnant. Life was good—for a while.

◆ ◆ ◆

I get up to stretch my legs, but there's nowhere for me to

go, so I pull a paper cup from the water cooler and fill it. I didn't know these old water coolers were still around. It's the kind with cone cups. What are you supposed to do with a cone-shaped cup? You can't even set it down anywhere.

I'm about to sit back down when the door opens. "Mr. Montgomery?" The detective calls my name and holds the door.

Beth and I exchange glances as we pass. I can't quite work out what she's thinking. I pause for a moment; I want to talk to her, but the detective speaks up again. "Right this way, Mr. Montgomery."

I follow the detective down the hall. He stops and points into a room. "Right in here."

I take the far chair, wondering if this is the same room that Kimber was in. She didn't even look at me when she walked out with Lizzy, but she didn't look at anyone. Her head was down, her eyes on the floor.

"Mr. Montgomery, I'm Detective Parker. It's been a long wait, I know." He offers, "Would you like some water?"

I lift the hand with the cup from the cooler.

"Right. Okay, we'll get right to it then." He flips his notebook to a fresh page. "As I understand from your wife, you are long-time friends with the victim."

No, I have never been his friend. "Yes, I have known him a long time."

"What time did you arrive at the party?"

"It was before 7:00, maybe 6:30. We came a little early."

He jots something down in his book. "Any particular reason?"

I rub my forehead. *More time with Kimber.* "It's silly, but I like to park in the driveway instead of the street. So, I wanted to get to the party before everyone else did."

"And what did you all do before the rest of the guests arrived?"

"We went out to the patio because the caterers needed to set up. We weren't out there very long. Then the other guests started to arrive."

A chill runs through me. It's so cold in here! I bet Kimber was freezing.

Parker rubs his knee and grimaces. "How much would you say you drank tonight?"

"I made myself a drink when we got there. Then I had another one shortly after that."

"Okay," he pushes back in his chair, "did you see anything tonight that stands out in your mind?"

Umm ... yeah, a fantastically dead Jake Carter. "No, nothing at all."

"Where were you when you heard Mrs. Carter screaming?"

"I was in the living area talking with Allie Carter and my wife." I'm already over this. Let me go home.

"Did you see anyone arguing tonight?"

"No."

"Did you go upstairs at any time?"

"No."

"Did you see anyone else go upstairs?"

"No."

"Is there anything else you think might be pertinent to this investigation?"

"No."

Detective Parker gets up from his chair, letting out a little grunt. "Okay, well, thank you for your time. I'll get someone to take you and your wife back to your car."

"Thanks. I appreciate it." We shake hands, and I walk back down the hall.

I find Beth waiting, looking a little lost. I extend my hand. "Come on, sweetheart. Let's go home."

CHAPTER THIRTEEN

Cindy

Night of the Murder 7:00 p.m.

"I don't want to go, Greg! Please!" My words come out ragged and shaky. I'm not used to raising my voice.

I'm arguing with my husband about this stupid work party at Jake Carter's big, fancy mansion. Mr. Carter is one of my new bosses at the law firm Martin & Carter, and he crossed the line with me. I won't go into the details, but what he did was more than a run-of-the-mill pass. No. What he did was sexual harassment.

I talked to my other boss, Mr. Martin, about it that same afternoon. I told him what happened with Mr. Carter, and he assured me nothing like that would happen again. I hope he's right. The pay there is twice as much as I ever thought I'd make, especially coming from a little town like Rabbit Hash.

Another loud bang comes from the kitchen. Greg is slamming things around. He's been looking forward to this event since I wrote PARTY AT MR. CARTER'S HOUSE on our kitchen calendar and circled it in red. How was I supposed to know Mr. Carter would turn out to be such a creep?

So, I've told Greg I have a headache and don't want to go to the party anymore. So now he's mad and throwing a little hissy fit. They call it *showing his tail* where I come from. He's just not being his best self.

I do understand why this party is important to him. Greg is in law school and wants to rub shoulders with some big-name practicing attorneys. Martin & Carter is a well-known and respected firm that brings in a *ton* of money. If Greg could get his foot in the door there—shoot. We would be set for life!

Greg hollers from the kitchen, "Cindy! Where the heck is the peanut butter?"

Ugh, "Stop screaming at me, Greg! It's still in the cooler."

We returned from a trip to the beach this morning. I had the whole week off of work with pay. Plus, Mr. Maritn let us use his two-bedroom oceanfront condo. Greg thinks the use of the condo and the time off with pay were all for a *job well done*. It's not exactly the truth, but what else was I supposed to do? If I told him what happened with Mr. Carter, he would want me to quit working there. There isn't a doubt in my mind. So, yeah. I had to *fudge* the truth a little bit.

Greg walks into the bedroom, all sulky and hanging his head. *Oh. This routine*. He's going to guilt me into changing my mind.

Mr. Pitiful takes a seat on the bed next to me. "Look," he says, taking my hand. "I'm *so* sorry you have a headache. I *truly* am," he alleges as he puts his hand over his heart. "But you know how much I want to go to this party. I've been counting down the days. Can't you take a Tylenol or something?" He runs his hand through his gorgeous blonde hair. "We don't have to stay too late. Please, Cin?"

Ugh. I look at my husband. If I don't give in, he will pout like a child for the rest of the evening, if not longer. Even if I know he's manipulating me, I cave. "Ok, fine," I say, irritated. "I guess I need to go and get ready."

Victory is written all over his handsome face. He puts his hands on my shoulders and kisses me. "Thanks, babe. Love you."

You love that you won. That's what you love! As I head into the bathroom, I make my position clear. "I'm not making any promises about how long we'll stay. You hear me, Greg? When I'm ready to go, that's it. I mean it." I check the time. "We're already late, you know."

Still grinning, he says, "It's fashionable to be late." A second later, he adds, "But, hurry up!"

CHAPTER FOURTEEN

Kimber: Part Three
Night of the Murder

I hurry to the door and find a mob of people peering back at me, not one familiar face among them. "Welcome," smile plastered. "Welcome, everyone! We are so glad you came." Each guest returns my smile as they file in. "Come right this way. We have food and refreshments in the kitchen. I'm Kimber. Jake is right in here." I feel a bit like a tour guide as I cross the foyer. On your left and right, you'll see my collection of blue and white china, and under this arch ...

These are Jake's soccer friends. A quick tally tells me there are five couples altogether. It's interesting that they have all arrived at the same time. They must have caravaned. I find that a little odd. Perhaps these kinds of people prefer to travel in packs.

It's a mixed lot. They are *all* underdressed, but one couple sticks out. The man is wearing a concert T-shirt, of all things, and his wife, a buxom blonde, is wearing flip-flops. Can you believe it? Who wears flip-flops to an evening party?

No matter. These people are my guests, and I intend to fuss over them the same as I would anyone else. The group fills the kitchen. I make sure each one of them finds their preferred refreshment. All the women choose wine: four whites and one red. Not unusual. The rough-looking fellow pours a healthy amount of bourbon into his glass. The rest of the men follow suit, except for the redhead, who also adds ice and ginger ale.

Guests continue to arrive. Eli, Jake's younger brother, and his wife, Allie, arrive next. Eli has the Carter family's good looks, but he's not as perfectly put together as Jake is. Still, he has stormy blue eyes and a similar athletic build. I'm sure that any woman would consider him attractive.

Eli wraps his arms around me. "How's it going, Sis?" He's called me "Sis" since the day I married Jake, and I love it.

"Wonderful, of course." I smile as I do. "What other way is there to be?"

I turn my attention toward Allie, who is *very* pregnant. "Oh, Allie, I can't wait to hold this little guy in my arms." I clasp my hands under my chin, "Auntie Kimber will be available for babysitting any time!" They have already settled on a name. Liam. It's perfect!

As they head for the food, the doorbell chimes again. I open the door, allowing Thomas and Caitlin to stroll in. Thomas is Jake's partner, and Caitlin is his lovely wife. They know the drill and make a beeline for the alcohol.

Let's see. That's almost everyone. If I remember correctly, we are still expecting the Prescotts. Cindy, the newest paralegal at the firm, and her husband.

Over the years, we have invited many paralegals to these

parties, but they seldom show up. I'm sure I can imagine why.

I settle at the island with Lizzy, Beth, and Allie, taking a moment to survey the room. The conversation is flowing, people are eating, and everyone seems content. Jake is in his element, regaling the group with stories of his many triumphs in all his inflated glory. Every one of them is hanging on to every word. Spellbound.

That's how it was for me all those years ago. I was drawn to Jake the moment we met. The attraction went beyond his face and well-developed muscles. Jake was the glittery thing, the shiniest bauble, the life of the party, the top dog in any setting. He was the drug, and I became an addict. The sex was a little rough, but I was okay with that. Jake filled my needs.

I'm pulled back to the present by Allie's laugh. She and Beth are talking about babies. I look across at Lizzy and see that she is lost in thought. Her brows are furrowed, causing two vertical lines between her eyes. *Nothing a little Botox wouldn't fix.* I would bet my Versace robe that she is worrying about Chloe.

Poor Lizzy looks for disaster around every corner when it concerns her only child. I know that Chloe going away to college will be challenging for Lizzy. But all mothers must come to terms with letting go. We have to watch our babies jump into deep waters, wringing our hands, anxious to see if they will sink or swim—all the while waiting on the dock with a life ring on each arm, just in case.

The conversation shifts from babies to Botox. I mention that I've been thinking about a mini-facelift. The girls are giving their opinions. I listen, but as they speak, I sense him coming. The hair on my arms rises, and my heart drops to my stomach.

Jake snakes his arm around me and puts his mouth next to my ear. He growls. His hot breath desecrating me in filth. "That dress makes you look like a fat cow. You're nothing but a used-up, dirty whore." I smile, nod, and keep going on as I always do. He kisses me on the forehead, smiles at the other ladies, and walks away as if he hadn't spewed his venom all over me.

This isn't a game, you know. Jake means every word he says, and he will show me his complete disgust later. I have been warned. It's coming—it's coming the minute we are alone.

I lock the dread away where it belongs and excuse myself to check on my other guests. I work my way through the room to where Eli and Collin are standing, my two favorite men on Earth. "Hello, boys! Can a girl join the conversation?"

Eli grins. "Sure, we were talking about carburetors." *He's teasing.*

Collin says, "And football."

I play along and scrunch my nose. "Okay, I can take a hint! I'm leaving!" I huff and turn around with great drama. Collin grabs my arm. "We're messing with you. We were talking about Eli's upcoming daddyhood. I was giving him some pointers."

"Such as?" I ask.

"I told him to volunteer for the nighttime feedings." Collin smiles.

I'm confused. "Allie is breastfeeding, isn't she?" I look to Eli, then to Collin, and back to Eli.

"Exactly!" Collin laughs, thinking he's hilarious.

I roll my eyes and punch him in the arm. "You're terrible!" We talk for a few more minutes before Eli excuses himself to go to the bathroom.

Collin leans in. "Come outside with me for a minute."

We push out into the night air. I already know what he wants to talk about. Collin is worried about me. He is *always* worried about me.

"So, how are you?" He starts.

I told you. "I'm fine, Collin. I am." It is so sweet that he cares, but he can't do anything for me. I'm a lost cause. I always have been.

"How are your bruises? Has he hit you again?"

"Collin, I told you that it's not like that. And my bruises are fine. They're almost gone."

"I hate that he does that to you. It's not right, Kim."

"Collin, that discussion is closed. I'm not talking about it anymore. It's not a big deal, and it's not a regular thing. This is why I never told you. I knew you would react this way."

"Of course I'm going to react this way." I can see the concern on his face, but he shifts gears. "Did you take any uppers today?"

"Collin, they aren't *uppers*. For Heaven's sake. It's not like crystal meth or something. It is a real prescribed medication."

He shoves his hands deep into his pockets. "Not prescribed to you, though."

"I'm careful with them, Collin. I promise. I don't take them every day. I only take them when I need to. And when I do, I only take them in the morning. I know you're not supposed to mix them with alcohol. So I don't. Okay?" I shift my weight in my Louboutin heels. "You know I have to have my wine at night." I smile sheepishly, trying to be coy and lighten the mood—unsuccessfully.

"What about your relaxers? You can't take those while you're drinking either. The two don't mix. You know that, right?" His tone is serious. "Promise me you won't mix them. I worry about you, Kimber. You have no idea."

"I do, and I love you for it, but you worry too much. All the worry in the world isn't going to fix me. You should know that by now." I trail his jawline with the back of my fingers. "I'll be careful. I promise. Okay?"

Collin kicks the ground and asks, "Did he buy you that bracelet? I've never seen it before. It's beautiful on you."

I look at the bracelet, its diamonds sparkling in the moonlight, and remember the night I paid for it. "Yes, he did." *Sort of.* "It's sweet you noticed. Most men don't notice those kinds of things." I add, "Beth is a lucky girl to have you, Collin."

His look is sharp. I know exactly where his mind is. I shouldn't have said that. Before he has a chance to say anything, I speak first. "We should get back inside. I am the hostess, after all." I touch the tips of his fingers with mine, letting them linger there for a minute before interlocking fingers. I give him a tug. "Come on, let's go back inside."

As we are going back in, I see that new guests have arrived. *Oh no.* I race in to save them from Lizzy. I do my usual flight of air kisses and greet them. "Oh my gosh, welcome! I'm Kimber, Jake's wife. You must be Cindy," I say, dripping with hospitality, and turn to her husband. "And Greg, right?" I beam. "Let's go get you something to drink."

I watch them as they make their choices. The girl is a knockout. I bet my husband has already made a run at her. If he hasn't, he will soon. Her husband, Greg, still has some bulking up to do, but I can tell he will fill out nicely when he does. They seem like a sweet couple. I say a quick prayer, asking that Jake will leave her alone, but I know it's in vain. Jake doesn't answer to God. Jake Carter is the devil himself.

CHAPTER FIFTEEN

Lizzy: Part Two
Night of the Murder

More guests roll in. Kimber helicopters around everyone, ensuring every guest feels welcome and is attended to. I have come to the conclusion that she lives for these parties. She never looks happier than she does when she has a house full of guests. Hospitality seems to be Kimber's special talent.

I sit on my perch at the island, watching the party unfold. I claim this island for my own at every Carter event. It's the perfect place for me to be nosey without being noticed. A person can learn so many things by simply observing.

I can tell you right now that something is going on with one of the soccer men and a wife. Not *his* wife, mind you, but the wife of his teammate. They are throwing all kinds of signals: sideways glances, coy smiles, and unnecessary touches. *Oh my gosh.* Now she is flipping her hair. *Oh, yes.* Something is going on. Mark my words!

Another perk of the island is that I can be cordial without being overly social. Party-goers flow in and out of the kitchen as they get another plate or refill their glasses. Each one upholds their duty to make small talk with me as they waft into my area. Tonight, even the stocky man manages a hello.

I appreciate that we all have to play by the rules. In society, we do what people expect of us. If someone sneezes, you bless them. If you cross in front of someone in the grocery aisle, you say, Excuse me. If you have to cough, you cover your mouth. These are simple things that everyone can do. Without these unwritten social rules, we might as well be living in a cave!

While I'm busy spying, a very round Allie bellies up to the counter and struggles to mount a bar stool. She manages to hoist herself up, puffing her hair away from her face. Breathy words push their way out. "Hey, Lizzy. How are things going?" Allie grabs a crostini. Her fifth plate, I believe. *Not that I'm counting.*

"Oh, you know, I can't complain. John and I are gearing up for Chloe to go away to college in the fall." Allie nods as she takes a bite. I ask, "How are you feeling, hon? Are you nervous about the delivery?"

Allie hurries to swallow. She puts up the one-minute finger and makes exaggerated chewing motions. After a gulp, she says, "I'm not too worried about the delivery. I mean, women have been giving birth since the beginning of time, right? My main thing is that I want to go into it with *super* positive energy."

I nod. *Positive energy. Ha!*

"I am a little worried about shedding this weight after the baby is born." Allie pats her substantial baby bump. "I have been absolutely ravenous. My doula says I have gained a few more pounds than I was supposed to. But I've already signed up for baby and mom pilates classes." She grins, pleased with herself, and takes another bite.

"Oh, pilates. That sounds like fun." *Pilates? Oh my gosh.* Is this woman prepared at all for the debilitating exhaustion that's coming with her new baby?

Allie reaches for a deviled egg, and I take the opportunity to check over the room again. The soccer buddy group has moved to the living area, commandeering Kimber's beautiful ivory couches. Jake, of course, is in the thick of them, holding court. Waves of laughter come from the group at regular intervals. Jake Carter is charismatic. I'll give him that.

Beth and Kimber join Allie and me at the island.

"Oh my God, Beth! Have you tried the goat cheese crostini? They are heaven!" Allie raves. "And the Cuban sliders, so good! Oh my God! Too bad I can't wash it down with some wine." Her lower lip protrudes in a pout.

"When is the baby due?" Beth asks.

Allie, caught again with a mouth full of food, mumbles, "Three more weeks." Instinctually, Allie's hand goes to her belly, as every mother does when her thoughts turn to her unborn baby. "We've chosen a birthing center as opposed to the hospital. They have a laboring tub if that's what I feel like, and I would like my family to be there. The center will allow me to have as many people as I want in the room. I'm hoping it will be a spiritual experience. Like, completely zen. I plan to go all-natural…."

Allie keeps talking about her birthing plans, and I take an unfortunate wrong turn down memory lane. Little nuggets of Chloe's life flood in. I would give anything to relive all those early years.

The first few days after they're born, all you can do is stare at them, amazed that you made this perfect little person in your *own* body. Of course, so many magical things follow: smiling, cooing, toddling—all the firsts. Those precious moments run through your fingers like golden grains of sand. Then they're gone. Just, gone.

It's been hard to watch Chloe grow up. Being a mom has been my whole world, and I can feel it slipping away. I'm not the center of Chloe's life anymore. I don't think she even has me in the same stratosphere. My baby girl is shedding me like an old skin that doesn't suit her anymore. Feeling the prick of tears, I swirl my wine around my glass and let my voice of reason speak.

"To be completely honest," lectures my voice of reason, pretending to be me, "I don't want to raise another child. The mere thought of it is exhausting. It's ridiculous, a woman of my age! Why would I put myself through all of that again? I would have to be insane!" The lies do their job, if only for the moment, and I return my attention to the conversation.

It has somehow shifted from babies to Botox. Kimber is talking. "I don't know where I'd be without Botox and fillers." She lifts her glass. "Cheers to Botox!" The rest of us cheer to Botox with an eye roll and a giggle.

Kimber has always admitted that she gets cosmetic injections. And she continues to sing their praises. "It's worth it. Sure, needles are scary for some people, but it makes a real difference." She adds, "I've been thinking about getting a little facelift."

Beth makes a face. "Kimber, you are one of the most

beautiful women I have ever seen. You put all the rest of us to shame!"

I add my two cents. "Beth is right, Kimber. If I had your face, I wouldn't let a scalpel anywhere near it." I want her to hear me. "I'm not joking, Kimber. You are gorgeous." I can see in her eyes that she doesn't believe me. Why can't she see it for herself?

As we speak, Jake waltzes up to Kimber as if on cue to reassure her how breathtaking she is. He slides an arm around her waist. We all watch as he whispers something in her ear. Sweet nothings, I assume. Kimber slides a graceful hand down her neck, smiles, and continues the conversation. "Beth, how are the kids?"

"Oh, the kids are doing great. They all finished with straight A's across the board." She continues, "Eliza has her first boyfriend."

Kimber gestures towards me with a thrust of her wine glass. "Must be something in the air." She says, "Lizzy's daughter has found love as well."

I interject. "No, no. It's not love, definitely not. It's a schoolgirl infatuation. Girls that age are so hungry for attention. Whenever a boy shows them a little, it's love."

"I agree," Allie responds as she shoves another egg in her mouth.

Beth, feeling defensive, rebuts, "We've met Eliza's boyfriend. He seems like a very genuine young man."

Kimber excuses herself to socialize. "I'll be back, ladies. I have my duties." We all watch Kimber walk away, envying her figure.

Allie comes up for a breath. "What's everyone doing for summer? Any trips planned?"

Beth speaks up. "Collin and I are planning to drive up the West Coast. It's something we've always wanted to do. My parents agreed to come and stay with the kids. We haven't taken a trip without the kids for years—not a *proper* trip anyway. We have only had a few nights now and again." She beams. "I'm super excited about it!" I watch as her expression changes. She adds softly, "I think we need the time away."

I follow her eyes and see Collin guiding Kimber onto the patio, his hand placed on the small of her back. My eyes return to Beth, who has lost her color. *Oh, dear.*

"Beth, it looks like you are out." I point to her empty wine glass. "We can't have that!" I touch one of the wine bottles. "Which one are you having?" She points to the pinot noir, and I fill her up.

No, wine doesn't solve anything, but sometimes it helps smooth the rough patches.

CHAPTER SIXTEEN

Cindy
8:30 p.m.
Night of the murder

I step up to the Carter's enormous front door, feeling a lot like Alice in Wonderland, dwarfed in a world of giant-sized things. I push the doorbell and wait. Greg knocks. Nothing.

Okay! Works for me. "Well, guess the party's over. Let's go back home."

"Not a chance, sweetheart." Greg opens the door himself and nudges me through.

Whoa. It really is Wonderland. *Crap.* We don't belong here. I want to turn around and go back home.

Greg, on the other hand, is thrilled. He takes my hand and squeezes it. "I bet you're glad we came now, huh?"

"Nope."

Greg gives me the side-eye. "Come on, party pooper. It will be fun. Let's get you a drink." He takes my hand and pulls me deeper into the house.

We follow the noise into a large living area. I'm relieved to see so many people. I was worried it would be a more intimate setting. If we're lucky, we won't have to talk to Mr. Carter at all.

Greg and I are standing here taking it in, unsure of what to do when a woman comes to greet us. I assume it is Mrs. Carter, but she doesn't look like I pictured her. She isn't the beautiful, refined woman I envisioned.

"Hi, I'm Lizzy, the neighbor," she says.

Oh, so not Mrs. Carter. I start to say something to the neighbor when a woman who looks *exactly* as I imagined comes flying at our faces. She makes kissy noises on each side of my head. I'm not sure if I'm supposed to make kissy noises back. But if I was, it's already too late.

After complimenting my dress, Mrs. Carter guides us into the kitchen. She introduces us to the round of people there. I'm anxious for a drink. Greg pours himself a whisky and Coke, then opens a bottle of Chardonnay for me. He hands me a full glass. I search the faces in the room, looking for Mr. Carter. I spot him talking with a group of men in the living room.

It takes ten seconds for my body to double-cross me. The blood rushes to my face, and I turn into a tomato. I try to blame it on the wine, even though I have yet to take a sip. Flushing is something that happens to me when I'm anxious. I'm convinced it's a curse, even if I don't know what I did to deserve it. Momma says it's just my cross to bear.

I do a quick outfit check of the women around the island. They are all wearing cocktail dresses. I fit right in. I take a thankful sip of wine and then another. This is the best wine I have ever had! So much better than what I drink at home. I make a mental note to check the bottle for the name before we go.

A few awkward minutes go by before Mr. Martin comes over and introduces himself to Greg. The men shake hands before he turns to me, "You look lovely, dear." His eyes are so kind, but it does little to calm my nerves. I guess that's what the wine is for—I take another sip.

Mr. Martin gestures for us to come with him. "I'd like you both to come and meet my wife."

Mrs. Martin is another elegant, poised woman. She looks like a first lady to me. I get a sharp prick of anxiety, and self-doubt sinks into my stomach. Again, I want to go home. These women are out of my league. I feel like a little girl playing dress-up.

"Darling," Mr. Martin says to his wife, "I would like you to meet Cindy Prescott and her husband, Greg."

The first lady extends her hand. "Thomas has told me so many splendid things about you." Her voice is soft and velvety. "Promise you'll tell me if he makes you work too hard." Mrs. Martin touches my arm. "I'm always telling him that even at work, he should live a little. Go ahead, take a little extra time for lunch, and come home early every now and then. It can't be all work, work, work." She oozes refinement. "Thomas tells me you have a little one."

Mrs. Martin continues with questions about our daughter: How old is she? Are we planning on having any more? Have we thought about private schools? As we talk, I can feel the anxiety falling away. I'm not sure if it's the conversation or the wine. Maybe both. Whatever the reason, even my toes don't feel so pinched in these outrageously uncomfortable heels.

Greg reaches over and takes my empty glass. The first one has gone straight to my head, and the wine speaks up for the first time tonight.

"Yoo-hoo, ya feeling me yet?" Lady Alcohol asks.

I try to ignore her and focus on the conversation. Mrs. Martin is talking to me about a book club her daughter-in-law belongs to. "Her name is Marcy. She's a little bit older than you, but the two of you would hit it off. Do you read much? I love a good murder mystery."

Greg returns with our drinks and addresses Mr. Martin. "I want to thank you so much for recognizing Cindy's hard work. Giving her the week off with pay and the use of the condo was amazing. The weather was awesome the whole week. We had a great time." Greg grins from ear to ear. *Oh no.*

Mrs. Martin raises an eyebrow at Mr. Martin, who then raises an eyebrow at me. The gesture was barely perceptible. Luckily, Greg didn't seem to notice. Mr. Martin speaks up. "Yes, well, she earned it. She does exemplary work."

Oh God, my face was still recovering from the last time. I bury myself in my glass of wine.

"Greg," Mr. Martin begins, "Cindy tells me you are in law school."

Greg perks up. This is what he's been waiting for. I listen to him talk with Mr. Martin for a while before feeling a hand on my shoulder. All of my hair stands on end. *Get your hands off me.*

Mr. Carter inserts himself into the group. "Cindy! I'm so glad you could make it! And this must be your husband." He reaches out to Greg and says, "Jake Carter, nice to meet you! I've heard so much about you." *Lies! I have never talked about anything but business.*

Mr. Carter turns back to me. "Cindy has brightened up our

office. You're a lucky devil." Mr. Carter winks at me as he says it. He *winks* at me! The nerve of this man! I catch Mrs. Martin's eye. She saw it too. The expression on her face is pure disgust. She knows exactly what kind of man Jake Carter is.

"You two enjoy yourselves." Mr. Carter flashes a cat-ate-the-canary smile at me and says, "Mi casa. Su casa." He points double-finger guns in our direction before walking away.

I look at Mr. Martin. His expression is apologetic. A thread of fear strings through me. What if Mr. Martin can't keep his promise to me? What if Mr. Carter won't leave me alone? I push the thoughts to the back of my mind. With any luck, our interactions with him are over, and everything will be as it should come Monday.

It isn't long before my glass is empty again. I nudge Greg and show it to him. He nods, and we excuse ourselves to the kitchen for refills. I fill my glass to the top and hear Greg asking Jake's wife if it's alright for him to smoke out back. It's sweet that he asked, but I hate when he smokes. He has cut back a lot since we had Ginny. But he still has the occasional cigarette, especially when he's drinking.

Standing here alone, I'm feeling a little lost, so I busy myself perusing the food. I'm not hungry, but I need something to fill this awkward space. Besides, I haven't eaten since breakfast. When I'm nervous about something, I lose my appetite completely.

I choose an apple hand pie. The crust is a beautiful golden brown. I hope the filling includes cinnamon. My taste buds are primed for a sweet treat, but when I bite into it, there is no cinnamon, and there are no apples. I'm stuck with a mouthful of beef. *Oh, barf.* The green pukey face emoji flashes in my brain. *Cindy, you have to chew it up and swallow it. It's your only choice. The neighbor is sitting right beside you. A lady doesn't spit out her food.* I chew it up like a good girl, swallow it, and send half of my wine chasing after it.

I abandon the rest of the pie on the counter and top off my glass with what's left in the bottle of Chardonnay. *Oh boy.* I hope I'm not the only one who's been drinking from this bottle, but I'm pretty sure it's all me. The name on the label says Red Shoulder Ranch. I want to remember it so I can look it up later. *Red Shoulder Ranch, Red Shoulder Ranch, Red Shoulder Ranch*

When I look up, I see Greg torpedoing in my direction. "Come with me!" He grabs my wrist and drags me into the foyer, the wine sloshing around in my empty stomach and nearly out of my glass. "Greg! Have you lost your mind? What on Earth are you doing?" I wrench my arm away.

"You weren't going to tell me?"

Uh oh. My best bet is to pretend I don't know what he's talking about. I mean, he could be talking about something else, right? "Tell you what?" I take a big gulp of my wine.

"Cindy, I was outside and overheard them talking about you."

Still hoping he isn't talking about what I think he is, I ask, "Who?"

Greg's eyes are wild. "Your two bosses, that's who! That asshole laid his hands on you. I'm going to kill him! Cin, I'm going to kill him."

Crap! He is *pissed*. This is bad, so bad. His face is now the same shade of red as mine. "Greg, I didn't tell you because I knew you would freak out, and evidently, I was right." *How detailed was the conversation on the patio?* "Nothing happened. He didn't get anywhere. I promise." Greg is on the verge of boiling over. I take his hand in mine. "Mr. Martin will take care of it. He promised it would never happen again. Please calm down."

I watch my husband's face as the penny drops. He jerks his hands away. "Oh my God! You lied to me! You said the trip and money were for," he makes air quotes, "a job well done! But it was really a pay-off." His voice is getting louder and louder. "Right?"

"Please, let's not do this here. Let's go."

"No! I'm going to confront the son of a bitch. You're my wife! This is bullshit!"

"Please, Greg, keep your voice down. Take a breath and think this through. This job could be a real opportunity for us. It could get you in the door to join the practice once you graduate. Mr. Martin said he would take care of it. We have to trust him for now. Jake Carter is a disgusting pig. He's one of those men who act that way with anything in a skirt. He doesn't care about me. Did you see his wife? She's beautiful."

His face softens. "You're beautiful."

I can see his brain working. I'm getting somewhere.

Finally, he says, "You're right. Let's go back in and schmooze with Mr. Martin. He's already on our side. I heard how he laid into the dickhead. Down the road, he could be my ticket in. Screw Jake Carter!"

Thank God. I take his hand as we work our way towards the Martins. They are talking with another couple.

"Cindy!" A broad smile comes across Mr. Martin's face. "Let me introduce you to Eli and Allie Carter."

Carter?

"This is Jake's brother Eli and his lovely wife, Allie." He smiles at the pair of us. "It is my honor to introduce you to our newest star, Cindy, and her husband, Greg. Greg is in law school. He is going to be an A-1 lawyer one day."

I get the sense Eli is nothing like his brother. "So nice to meet you both," I say as I admire Allie's round baby belly. My hand, on auto-pilot, goes straight for it. *Cindy!* "Oh my gosh, I'm so sorry. I'm sure you don't want some stranger's hand on your baby—your belly—your baby belly." *Gosh darn wine!*

Allie responds, "I don't mind at all. Pregnancy is a beautiful, natural part of life. It's normal to touch another woman's body when she's carrying a child. It ties us all together. In some ways, we are all the same woman."

Lady Alcohol continues running commentary inside my head. "Ha Ha Ha! She's a hippie. That's beautiful, man."

I ignore what I'm hearing. "Oh, that's a great way to think about it. I get what you mean. Is this your first baby?"

She nods. "Yep, first one. I've got three weeks to go. I'm so ready!"

"We have a daughter. She'll be two in July." I see the shock in her expression. It's not unusual. We are young parents. "It was one of those happy accidents, but I wouldn't change a thing."

Allie's expression is so sweet. "Of course you wouldn't. Babies are *always* a blessing." She cocks her head and says, "Can you give me any tips?"

It is a rare occasion that anyone asks me for advice. Two

words fly out of my mouth: "The vacuum." *Ta-da.* I say it proudly, as if I invented the wheel.

Allie raises both eyebrows and waits for me to elaborate. "My Ginny was a big ole fusspot in the beginning. That baby cried no matter what I did. I thought I was the worst mother ever. Meanwhile, the house was a total disaster. One day, I put her in the swing and pulled out the vacuum."

My heart warms at the memory of my red-faced angel with her tiny baby fists in little balls. Screaming at the top of her lungs in the baby swing. "When I turned the vacuum on, she was quiet, but when I turned it off, she screamed. It was like magic." I wiggle my fingers in the air, "like a serious voodoo kind of magic." I take a swig, "Be careful, though. I burned a hole in my carpet by letting it run too long." Another swig. "You need to lean it back so the roller isn't touching the floor. Like this." I demonstrate by leaning back an invisible vacuum.

The corners of Allie's mouth turn up. "Wow. That's—good to know!"

While Allie tells me about her birth plan, the men excuse themselves to refill their drinks. Greg doesn't need another drink. We still have to drive home. Besides, his jealousy goes to another level when he overdoes it. It was nothing short of a miracle that I talked him down before.

Mrs. Martin joins back in the conversation. I listen to her and Allie talk about the benefits of midwifery for what seems like forever. *Uh oh.* I'm losing track of time. That's when I know I've had too much to drink.

Lady A. bubbles up again. "*That's* when you know you've had too much to drink, Miss Voodoo Magic?"

Mr. Martin returns to us, but Greg isn't with him. I turn my head to look for him, but the room begins to spin. I'm feeling very drunk all at once. I excuse myself from the group. I don't see Greg anywhere. Maybe he went for another smoke. I look through the glass door to the patio, but he's not out there either. Paranoid, I scan the kitchen and living room for Mr. Carter. He seems to be missing too.

I'm swaying in my painful designer heels when I hear these awful, blood-curdling screams. Everyone around me rushes to the foyer, chasing the noise. And I'm carried along with them like a leaf in a stream.

We all find Mrs. Carter looking down at her husband with her hands over her mouth. Mr. Carter lies splayed across their beautiful floor with a knife sticking out of his chest. His eyes are wide open, and his neck is bent.

It sinks in. He's dead. Jake Carter is dead.

Lady A. pitches her piece of coal in the fire, "Oh, yeah! Dead. Dead. Dead. Hiccup. Dead as a fricking doornail."

I'm startled by fingers curling around my arm and almost lose my footing. It's Greg. He's white as a ghost. I look at my husband and back at Mr. Carter. Could Greg have done this?

No ...

He couldn't.

I hope not!

Oh my God!

Maybe he did!

CHAPTER SEVENTEEN

Lizzy: Part Three
Night of the Murder

While trying to keep Beth occupied with conversation, a new couple strolls in from the foyer. I don't recognize them. They are both beautiful people in their early twenties, standing there looking lost. The supreme hostess with the mostess is still outside with Collin.

I hop off my stool and attempt to fill in for Kimber, trying to match her enthusiasm. "Hi, I'm Lizzy, the neighbor." As I hear them leaving my mouth, I regret my words. *Hi, I'm Lizzy, the neighbor?Good Grief.*

Before I can recover, Kimber flies in, air kissing them on both sides of their faces. "I'm thrilled you could make it. It's so wonderful to finally meet you!"

The girl is dumbstruck.

"Cindy, right? Oh, my God. Your dress is to *die* for." Kimber draws out the word *die* for impact.

No longer needed, I reclaim my stool as Kimber guides the

couple into the kitchen. "Ladies, this is Cindy and Greg Prescott. Cindy is working with Jake." Kimber rattles off our names, and we all throw a smile or a wave.

Introductions over, the husband pours whiskey and Coke for himself. His young wife chooses the chardonnay, he pours her a generous glassful. She's an attractive girl. Her dark hair is pulled into an updo with little wispy tendrils tugged loose. The husband, Greg, hasn't grown into himself yet; his body is still more boy than man, but I can see the potential.

Kimber is aglow in her hostess sunshine. "Jake mentioned you were on vacation last week. Fun in the sun?"

"Oh, umm, yes," Cindy says. "We took a short trip to Florida. Destin. It was nice to get away." Her eyes flit around the room and finally settle on Jake. I watch as the heat flushes her face. Feeling it, she presses her glass against her cheek, seeking relief. Cindy turns her attention back to Kimber, aware of her gaze. "It's the wine," the girl lifts her glass. "It colors me every time. It's so embarrassing."

The wine, huh? I take another sip of my own.

"Don't be silly," Kimber soothes. "It's barely noticeable. I have an aunt who is the same way. Besides, you've just returned from Florida. Your face is sun-kissed!" Kimber raises her glass toward Cindy and says, "To Florida!"

Everyone around cheers, "To Florida," including me. *All hail the toastmistress!*

Thomas, Jake's business partner, approaches the young newbies. "Greg, is it? Nice to meet you." He drives his hand toward Greg, and they share a hearty shake. "Cindy here is a great asset to our office. We are thrilled to have her join the team." Thomas turns to Cindy, placing a hand on her shoulder. "You look lovely, dear. I'd like you both to come and meet my wife." Cindy produces the faintest of smiles and reluctantly follows Thomas toward his wife. I'm not sure what's going on, but this girl looks like she'd rather be anywhere else. My phone dings. It's a text from Chloe.

Chloe: Mom, have you been going through my things?
Me: No. Why would I be going through your things?
Chloe: I can tell things have been moved.
Me: Like what?
Chloe: Things in my drawer and my closet.
Me: Like what?
Chloe: MOM, JUST THINGS!!!
Me: Well, I didn't go through anything. I'm enjoying the party. We can talk about it later.

I turn my phone off and wonder how she knows. I was so careful to return things as I found them. At least, I *thought* I was careful. *Oh, Lizzy! Can't you ever do anything right?*

Crap. Now I need to come up with a plausible explanation for why Chloe's things aren't as they should be. I peer into my wine for answers. *Let's see.* Here's one. "I saw the cat in your room, Chloe. Lord knows what she could have gotten into. You know how crazy she can be." *It's not my best.*

I try another. "It must have been the exterminators. I saw a mouse the other day and called them out. Those men were all over the house, getting into every nook and cranny." *Not terrible.*

Maybe complete denial. "Chloe, you are being paranoid. Why

on earth would I go through your room?" *Humph.*

I'm leaning toward the exterminator when a stroke of genius comes over me—a cat/exterminator/denial combo. "The other day, I saw the cat chase a mouse into your room. I called the exterminator because there's never only *one* mouse. So, it could have been the cat, the exterminator, or a mouse. It certainly wasn't me!" *Winner, winner, chicken dinner!* I take a celebratory swig.

Satisfied that my problem is solved, I scan the room, taking stock. The soccer group has split, and the wives have broken off. Here comes the one wearing the sundress and flip-flops for another refill. Glass number five. *Not that I'm counting.* She stumbles and grabs the back of a stool to steady herself, but she continues on and pours another full glass of wine.

Only one of the soccer wives has not returned for a second glass. I believe her name is Susan. She's the wife of the ginger. *The designated driver, or an early pregnancy, perhaps?*

The young couple drifts back into the kitchen. The wife's face is still pained. She tips the bottle, refilling her glass to the very top. So much so that she has to slurp some from the edge so it doesn't slosh out when she moves. She sees me watching and shrugs her shoulders with a little smirk. I return her smile, trying to convey, "It's okay, honey. We've all been there."

The husband, Greg, asks Kimber's permission to go outside and smoke. *That's sweet.* I watch him go out onto the patio. He stands by the pool for a minute before disappearing out of sight.

His young wife is staring at the food. Is she waiting for one to pop up and offer itself to her? Finally, choosing an empanada, she takes the stool next to mine. I smile, but another roar comes from the soccer men, redirecting my attention. I look, expecting to see Jake at the heart of them, but instead, I see Jake and Thomas going out to the patio. *That's unusual.*

I continue watching them through the glass, wishing I could read lips. Thomas is very animated, with both arms flailing around. Jake appears wholly unruffled by the conversation. He slaps Thomas on the back and strides inside with his usual swagger. Thomas follows, brow furrowed, hankie out, blotting sweat from his forehead. It's obvious that he is flustered.

Greg comes in right after, looking much the same, heading straight for his wife. He grabs her wrist and pulls her into the foyer. *What is going on tonight?* Unfortunately, I can't see the couple from my seat. But they are only gone for a few minutes before rejoining the party. Whatever the problem was, it seems they have worked it out.

I'm watching Kimber talking to one of the soccer wives when one of the soccer husbands drifts my way, it's the redhead. To no one in particular, he says, "It all looks pretty good." Then he looks at me. "Any suggestions?"

"Oh, you can't go wrong. Everything is good. My favorite is the crab, though."

"Ah, that's my luck. I'm allergic to shellfish." He grins and says, "I'm Julian. This house is something else." He picks up a crostini and takes a bite.

"It's beautiful, isn't it? My name is Lizzy." He's not a bad-looking man. I sit up a little straighter. Not that I would ever be unfaithful to John, but a little flirting can lift your spirits.

I prepare myself for some playful banter, but one coy smile from me and two crostini-finishing bites later, Julian says,

"Well, it was good to meet you, Lizzy."

And just like that, I let go of my little balloon and watched it buzz around the room.

Luckily, I'm not deflated for long, because here comes Eli. I start the conversation as he refills his glass. "So, the big day is fast approaching! Are you guys ready to have your lives turned upside down?"

He laughs. "Well, I sure hope so. This baby is coming, whether we are ready or not. I hope it's sooner rather than later. I can't wait to meet my boy."

God bless him. I have always felt a little bad for Eli. He is so sensitive and tender-hearted. Growing up in the swath of Jake's giant shadow must have been hard.

"You're going to make the best dad, Eli. That baby is so lucky to have you and Allie." I add, "If you ever need a babysitter, don't hesitate to ask." I would love nothing more than to see five chubby little fingers wrapped around one of mine.

Allie comes into the kitchen and pokes her husband on the shoulder. "Hey, you left me," she teases.

Eli turns to her and says, "I would never leave you." He takes her face in his hands, tucks a stray piece of hair behind her ear, and kisses her. It's such a tender exchange that I'm almost embarrassed to be here. They both turn to me full of love, and my heart feels so full I could cry. *Wait. What?* How much have I had to drink? My eyes go from my empty glass to the empty bottle, and I nod. *Ah, Yes. I see.* Too much wine makes me sappy.

The lovebirds wander off, and I am left alone again to surveil. Jake is headed to his office with one of his soccer buddies in tow. He makes the same pilgrimage at each party, but this is the first time he's ever taken someone with him.

Years ago, I followed him to see what he was doing. I saw him shake cocaine out of an envelope, cut a line with a razor blade, and snort it up his nose through a straw. I watched him do two lines before sneaking away. He had no idea that I was there, watching him. No one ever does.

I survey the remaining food. There is only one lonely crab croquette left. It would be such a shame if it went to waste. After all, Kimber pays a lot of money for this gourmet food. In the spirit of not wasting decent food or decent money, I pull the last bit of crab home to Mama. I swear, I could live on these things.

I'm still licking Remoulade off my fingers when I see Jake returning from his office—sniffing hard and pinching his nose. He comes into the kitchen and pours another drink, number five. *Not that I'm counting.* We exchange a few words before he returns to the pack.

My island is deserted.

CHAPTER EIGHTEEN

Kimber: Part Four
Night of the Murder

I've spent the better part of my life groping around in the darkness, looking for answers—answers to explain why I feel the things I feel and do the things I do. But those answers would never be found, because they weren't there in the first place.

The only thing I found in that deep, drawing, darkness was Jake. He was waiting for me in the pitch, ready to gobble me up—and gobble me up he did.

I suppose it's time to tell you all of it.

As I said earlier, we play pretend. We go on lovely vacations. Jake buys me lavish gifts and, most of the time, acts like he loves me. To outsiders, he puts on like he is the luckiest man in the world to have me, and everyone buys it. *Everyone.* But it's all a show.

If you look closely—really look—the truth is in Jake's eyes. I think it's always been there and I suppose that may be what drew me to him in the first place. Can it be that I sought out someone who hated me more than I did and then pulled them close? It seems that's exactly what I did.

My memories of that first episode are vivid. Calling them *episodes* is easiest for me. They sound more clinical that way. Something akin to a seizure. I guess it's a coping mechanism. Our brains are remarkable, aren't they? They find the strangest ways to keep us going.

It was very late on a Friday night. Jake's footsteps fell heavy on the stairs. I was awake as he entered our bedroom but remained still. Eyes closed. Feigning sleep. I listened as he removed his cuff links, setting them with a clink on the nightstand. I expected to hear him close the bathroom door and then start the shower. Instead, he crawled into bed and straddled me. I was confused. It had been ages since he wanted sex from me.

I kept my eyes shut, hoping that if I was still, Jake would leave me alone. Instead, he hung over me, his nose touching mine. His breath was hot, smelling of alcohol. He let out a low, ungodly snarl. It didn't sound human. My eyes flew open.

Jake's face was distorted. His eyes were black. I was in trouble.

He grabbed my throat with both hands and began to squeeze. I tried to push him away. I clawed at his fingers, desperate for them to release me, but it was a lost cause. My strength is nothing compared to Jake's. I remember thinking this was it. This is how I will die. I will be strangled to death—in my own bed—by my own husband.

Instead, Jake loosened his grip and then let go. My hand instinctively went to my throat, as if I could protect it. My whole body was shaking. Jake was hulking over me, looming like a storm. "You stupid bitch!" He drove his palm into my face as he pushed off the bed.

Jake threw off the covers. He ripped my nightgown from my body and did the same with my underwear. "Look at you!" His voice was full of contempt. "Your tits are disgusting." He slapped one breast with the back of his hand. "Roll over," he demanded. "So I don't have to look at them." I did as I was told.

Jake continued his assault. "Ha! Your fucking flabby ass! It makes me sick!" His open hand slammed down on my butt with all his strength. I sucked in the pain. I didn't know a slap could hurt so much. He did it over and over.

Jake screamed, "Do you know how lucky you are that I haven't left you?" They kept coming. "Why should I stay with an ugly cow like you?"

I begged him not to wake the kids. "Please, Jake ...." My eyes stung with hot tears. "The babies."

"Shut your mouth!" He moved to the bottom of the bed and yanked me by my ankles, pulling me toward him, and then spread my legs with his own. He lifted my hips to his level and drove hard into me from behind. I felt the warm blood trickle up my stomach as my skin tore.

I began to lose myself in the swirl of pain. I'm not sure how long it went on. At some point, Jake pushed my face into the mattress. I couldn't move any air. My mind went to my children. They were too young to be without their mother. As I began to black out, he yanked my head back by my hair. I gasped for air, taking big gulps like a fish out of water. He pounded on my buttocks and thighs with his closed fists. He punched me in the kidneys. He spit on me.

When he finally let me go, I scrambled to pull the covers back over myself. I wanted to hide the body he hated so much.

After one last revolted scowl, Jake turned and went inside the bathroom. As soon as the door clicked shut, I assessed the damage. My fingers probed my battered, bloody vagina. The tear was significant. I needed stitches, but how could I go to the hospital? What would I say?

I found my ripped panties on the bed and pressed them against myself, listening for the shower to turn on. Once it did, I pulled three more panties out of the drawer, putting them on over the already saturated remnant in my hand. I thought about how much it would hurt in the morning when I peeled the crusty, dried underwear away from my wound.

I threw on a T-shirt and sweats. *How could I lie next to him with anything less?* I rushed to change the bloody sheets, shoving the soiled ones deep into the hamper, and curled up on my side of the bed. Tears rolled down my face. I was still processing what happened to me. My stomach was turning in on itself, and vomit rose in my throat.

Let me be clear. Sex with Jake has never been an act of love. He manhandled me, pulled my hair, and slapped me around. *A little*. Sex wasn't about intimacy for either of us. He liked it rough, and honestly, I was okay with that. But it was *nothing* like this. Not even close.

I heard Jake turn off the water. *He's coming.* I squeezed my eyes shut and waited for the man who beat and raped me to climb into bed beside me. The bathroom door opened, and a cloud of steamy heat followed Jake into the room, settling over me like a blanket.

Within a few minutes, Jake's breathing changed as he fell

asleep, and relief washed over me. I survived the ordeal with no idea what brought it on. But my body ached. The pain in my back was significant. My vagina throbbed. I didn't fall asleep until Jake left the house in the morning.

I woke up when Josie and Cam found me in bed. "Mommy, why are you still sleeping?" Josie giggled as she jumped on the bed. "Silly Mommy! It's morning time! See?" She pointed at the window with her pudgy little finger.

The children were so little then. They were up and at 'em and needed their mom, but I needed some time. I was sore, bruised, and swollen. I tried to walk without letting on how much it hurt, but Josie could tell that something was wrong. "You're walking funny, Mommy. Do your feet have boo-boos?"

Sweet Josie. "What a clever girl you are! You're going to be a doctor when you grow up!" Josie beamed with pride. "I *do* have sore feet today. That's all. It's nothing to worry about, pumpkin."

I settled them in front of the TV. "When Mommy is done, I will make you chocolate chip pancakes—with extra chocolate chips." That was the best I could do. Thankfully, it turned out to be enough.

In the shower, I turned on the water and let it wash over my battered body, watching the pink water swirl down the drain—caustic flashes of the previous night leaving blistered lesions in my mind. I wanted to scrub away what happened, but everything hurt. Standing under the water and washing my hair was all I could manage.

It was late afternoon when Jake breezed in as I stood at the stove making pasta. He greeted me with flowers and kissed me on the forehead as he handed them to me. "How was your day, gorgeous?" It was as though the previous night hadn't happened.

"Fine," I say as evenly as I can. "My day was fine." That word sealed my fate and told him everything he needed to know. Me saying *fine* after what he did to me was as good as telling him it was acceptable for him to treat me that way. I don't know why I didn't yell and scream, why I wasn't gone when he came home, or why I didn't call the police. I chose to stay and take what he had to give me. All of it: the house, the money, the status, the degradation, and the pain.

So, that's how it began and how it has continued. I endure these episodes. For giving birth. For the effects of gravity. For the passage of time. Followed by easy-going conversation, terms of endearment, and kisses on my forehead.

Neither Jake nor I ever talk about the episodes. We pretend they don't happen. But please hear this. Don't think for a minute that I enjoy them in any way. This goes way beyond my self-harm tendencies. Yes, I have struggled over the years. I have done a lot of damage to my body for reasons I can't explain, but this—nobody deserves this. Not even me.

As the years have passed, the episodes have slowly escalated. I think back to what Jake whispered in my ear tonight. I don't know how I'll be able to take another punishment so soon. I need time to heal from the last one. They have never come so close together, and Jake has never spoken to me in that way outside the confines of an episode. I'm worried. At some point, Jake will go too far, and my body will succumb. It's a matter of time—maybe tonight.

If you haven't figured it out yet, the episodes are the reason for the hydrocodone. I save them for those painful days after. I hoard them as if they are gold. When the kids had their wisdom teeth removed, they got ibuprofen, and I got their pain pills. If my stash becomes too low and there is no other way, I show up at the ER with an unfortunate gash requiring stitches. I do what I have to do.

The thought of asking Killa if he could get them for me has crossed my mind more than once. But so far, I have decided against it. Right now, I save them because they are hard to get. But if I had unlimited access ... well, it would only become one more monkey on my back, and right now, I am chock-full.

The last episode, the thrashing that awarded me my new bracelet, happened last weekend. Jake had a working dinner scheduled with a new client. An up-and-coming country singer and his wife.

I Ubered to the posh downtown restaurant so Jake and I could ride home together. I was already sitting at the table, chatting with the clients, when I saw Jake coming through the door. I smiled and waved, then I caught his eye. The change in his face was almost imperceptible. No one else would have been able to spot it, but I'd seen it before and knew immediately. I was in for it.

Something about me isn't up to his standard. The entire dinner, I tried to guess. Was a hair out of place? Is it the dress? Can he tell that I weighed one and a half pounds heavier on the scale this morning? What have I done? I had no idea.

After dinner, Jake drove us home in silence. We pulled into the driveway, and Jake was the first to the door, opening it for me with a grin. A diabolical gesture that told me all I needed to know. I was going to pay for something, and it would be brutal.

As soon as I crossed the threshold, I sprinted for the bedroom. I knew there was no getting away, but I needed it to happen where it always happens. I don't want horrible memories all over the house. If they are confined to one room, I can manage them somehow.

Jake bounded after me, taking two steps at a time. He roared, "How dare you show up to a meeting with clients looking like a cheap whore?"

I made it a few feet past the bedroom door before Jake caught me. He grabbed me by both shoulders. His handsome face morphed into something monstrous. "What is it?" I whimpered, "Jake, I don't know what I did. Please. Tell me. I'll never do it again. I swear."

"Damn right, you won't. You disgusting bitch." He threw me into the bathroom. I went flying across the floor, hitting my head on the tub. Hard. "Show me where that fucking red lipstick is."

The lipstick. I wore it, especially for Jake. Red is his favorite color. *I should have known better than to try something new.* I managed to get to my feet and hand him the tube. He grabbed me by the hair and smeared the lipstick onto my face, making a freakish smile from one ear to the other. "Look at yourself," he snarled, forcing me to see myself in the mirror. "Do you see? That's what you looked like tonight!" Spit flew from his mouth like a wild animal. Then he pulled the lipstick across my neck as if he were slicing my throat. "This is what you deserve."

I struggled to get my words out. "I'm so sorry, Jake. I will never wear lipstick again." I don't let the tears come. It only enrages him more. "I thought you would be pleased. It's your favorite color." It was wasted breath, and I knew it. Once the onslaught of violence begins, there's no going back.

The following morning, once again, I assessed the damage. I looked over my shoulder into the mirror and saw the word *whore* written in red lipstick across my back. Jake has called me that name a thousand times. But seeing that word on my body, like a label, hurt as much as the bruises on my thighs or my swollen labia. It's because I know some truth lies in the word he scrawled on my skin.

Before Jake came along, I opened my legs for an untold number of men. Sometimes, more than one a night. I *was* a whore, and each time those memories bubble up, it's painful. But I suppose that was the point. Wasn't it?

I'm brought back to the present when young Greg asks me if he can go outside for a smoke. "Of course you can," I reply, watching him step out onto the patio before taking another look around the space. Everyone seems okay, so I move to socialize with the soccer people. I haven't gotten any of their names yet, at least not any that have stuck in my brain.

Taking an empty spot on the couch, I engage a delightful woman. Cecily, as it turns out. "It's so nice to meet you, Cecily. I'm afraid I haven't been able to make it to any of Jake's games." I cluck my tongue as if it's such a shame. "I'm always busy chauffeuring my kids around. Our Josie is on the recreational volleyball team, and Cam did wrestling this year."

Cecily replies, "Oh, I know how that goes. We have two boys, both into soccer. It's a never-ending thing. Isn't it?" She smiles and takes a sip of her wine. *White. The pinot grigio.* "Your house is beautiful, by the way. It could be in a magazine."

I wave my hand in the air. "Thank you, but it wasn't all me. I had the help of an interior designer. I pointed to things I liked, and she put them all together."

We chat for a bit longer before I continue to the rest of the group. So far, I've met Cecily, Joel, Susan, redhead Julian, concert tee George, and flip-flop Molly. I have committed them to memory.

Now, there are only two couples left. I spot one of the wives alone. I saw her interacting with her husband earlier this evening. They looked at each other like young lovers, despite being in their fifties.

I approach her. "Hello. I'm so glad you could make it tonight. I didn't get your name."

Her smile is warm. "My name is Angela. Thank you so much for having us tonight."

"Angela." *Got it.* "Pleased to meet you!"

She taps her husband on the back, and he turns around. Angela introduces us. "Kimber, this is my husband, Mark."

After the usual pleasantries, Mark begins rattling off about Jake. "I'll tell you, Jake makes the rest of us look terrible." He continues to sing Jake's praises. "Our team wouldn't be where it is if it wasn't for your husband! He is a *star* athlete. It's too bad you haven't seen him in action …." *Blah, blah, blah …*

I continue to smile and nod while looking around the room. It's been a while since I checked. Collin is smiling, his arm thrown over Beth's shoulders. Jake is having a chat with concert tee George. Lizzy is still in the kitchen. I watch her for a moment before pushing on with Angela and Mark. It turns out that Mark is a veterinarian. I've never been an animal person. I suppose they are okay outside. But I don't want them in my house. One beast is more than enough.

When Mark finally comes up for a breath, I excuse myself to find my husband, who has since left George. I discover his body in disarray on the marble floor Maria mopped this morning. I walk over and look down at Jake; one of my kitchen knives is stuck in his chest. I become aware of my screams but fail at silencing them. Seconds later, people begin crowding around me, and then—Collin. I only remember Collin.

CHAPTER NINETEEN

Julian Herring

MNPD Criminal Investigation Division

Homicide Unit

Well, this is certainly an unexpected turn of events for everyone. I'm sure no one saw this coming. I can't say I'm upset about it. Considering Jake has been screwing my wife.

After meeting with the PI that day, I did go to soccer practice and asked if I could join the team. I didn't have a plan, but I needed to see this guy in person. Curiosity, I guess. I learned pretty quickly that he was an egotistical asshole. He's a lot better-looking than I am, but looks aren't everything. At least they shouldn't be.

When he invited me to this party, I saw it as a chance to get even closer—a more personal peek into his life. It would be an opportunity to have Jake and Susan in the same room and see how they acted around each other. Would they exchange knowing glances? Would they flirt openly in front of me? I also wondered about his wife. Does she know? If she doesn't, should

I tell her?

Susan didn't want to go to the Carter's party. She's been complaining of nausea the entire week. I'm sure she was setting the stage for bailing out tonight. But I was determined. We would *both* be at that party tonight—NO, was not an option.

You should have seen Susan's face when I came home that evening and told her I had joined a men's soccer team. She was standing in the kitchen, putting clean dishes away. Her head whipped around. "You what?"

"I've been feeling a little stagnant lately. So, I thought I'd join a soccer league. It's an over-forties team." Immediately, panic shaded her face.

"Where?"

"Oh, it's in Brentwood. The team goes by the name of *Brentwood Bombers*."

Her color turned ashen. "Why would you go all the way to Brentwood?"

"Why not? It's not *that* far, and they have a great practice facility."

Susan threw her hands in the air. "It doesn't make any sense to me, but whatever."

When the alarm rang from the foyer, we ran along with everyone else. I watched Susan's face to see her reaction. She looked shocked initially, but then I thought I saw a glimpse of relief. Right now, she's flipping through a magazine. It doesn't look like grief to me.

We are here with everyone else at the police department, waiting our turn to be questioned. I saw Sol Parker come out and call the other people. He's a good guy who was dealt a bad hand with a car accident. The last time I saw him, he said his knee was worse than ever.

He's been through a lot, but we got his medical bills paid along with a small settlement. I know he used that money to get at-home care for his ailing mother. She was nearing the end of her days and wanted to stay in the home that she loved and die in a place where she was comfortable. And that's what happened. She died in her bed with her loved ones by her side. That money paid for round-the-clock nursing care for the last year of her life. That's the kind of guy Sol is. He's one of the good ones.

The door opens, and my friend calls me back. "Come on, Red. It's your turn."

We walk down the hall. "So," he starts, "I bet you never imagined I would be questioning you in a homicide case, huh?"

Actually, I have. "Never in a million years. This whole thing is crazy." I follow Sol into a room. He sits down. I take the other chair.

Sol leans back and stretches out his legs. "I have to say, man, I didn't peg you for a soccer guy."

"Oh, well. I'm not." I chuckle. "I joined two weeks ago. I need to get back in shape." I grab my love handle and jiggle it a little. "But soccer isn't for me. I don't think I'll go back."

He nods. "Alright. We'll get right to it. I know you're ready to get out of here." Sol tosses his notepad on the table. "Please tell me you saw something that can help me figure this shit out."

I shake my head. "No. I wish I could help you, but it seemed like a normal party, except for the fact that I've never been to a house that swanky. I can't begin to imagine having that kind of money. But otherwise, it was drinks, food, and conversation." I turn up my hands and shrug my shoulders. "I didn't see anything out of the ordinary."

"Yeah, that's the story I'm getting from everyone." He continues, "What about the soccer practices? Was there anyone on the team that didn't get along with Carter? Did you ever see him having words with any of the guys?"

"No, I didn't see anything like that. If anything, it was the opposite. All the guys sucked up to him. I guess because he was the best player." I shrug again. "He seemed like a jerk to me. Cocky." *Way too cock-y with my wife.*

"Did you talk to him very much during the party?"

"Not really. For the most part, he did all the talking. The rest of us were a bit of a captive audience."

"He sounds like a real piece of work."

I nod. *Was ...*

"Did you notice anyone missing for any length of time toward the end of the night? Someone from the soccer team?"

"I can't say I was keeping tabs, but our group stayed together for the most part. Of course, people were going back and forth for food and drinks—trips to the bathroom. You know, that kind of thing."

Sol covers a yawn. "Alright, Jules, I'm going to let you guys go home. Tell Susan if she saw anything to give me a ring. I've still got eight witnesses to talk to, and I'm spent."

"Will do. Hang in there, man."

Sol groans as he stands up. "I'll get someone to take you and Susan back to your car."

I stand and offer my hand. "Good luck figuring this out. It

sounds like you have a real mystery on your hands."

"You're telling me. Give Susan my love. We should all get together sometime soon." Sol opens the door and leads me back down the hall. His limp is pretty bad tonight. "Sit tight. I'll get you a ride."

I sit next to Susan and take her hand. She looks at me and smiles. "Love you, babe."

"I love you too." More than you'll ever know.

DEVIL IN THE PITCH

CHAPTER TWENTY

Thomas Martin
MNPD Criminal Investigation
Homicide Unit

I'm still reeling. My long-time friend and business partner was murdered tonight. I have to say, I'm not all that surprised Jake's life ended this way. In fact, it's been a constant worry of mine. But I never thought it would happen the way that it did—stabbed at his own party with a house full of people he invited to be there.

We've had more than one angry husband barge into our office, shouting threats and profanities in Jake's direction. I knew it would catch up with him one way or another. He was reckless in his behavior. One day, he was going to sleep with the wrong wife. I knew it.

But Jake never took any of it seriously. He felt invincible. No harm could ever come to The Mighty Jake Carter. And yet, he looked awfully dead tonight, lying at the bottom of the stairs. I'll never get his shocked expression on his face out of my head.

I glance at my watch. It's almost 1:00 a.m. We are all trapped in this airless room at the mercy of Metro PD. The soccer husbands and wives are propped up against one another, trying to sleep. Two of the men are snoring. My wife is picking polish off of her nails.

A police officer has been posted at the door, babysitting us all night. I have to say, his stamina is impressive. He has been standing with his hands clasped in front of him the entire time. He's hardly moved a muscle. *Admirable.* As for myself, I've been fidgety. I have loosened my tie, slouched in my chair, stretched out my legs, and adjusted my business multiple times.

The door swings open, and everyone turns with high hopes toward the man behind it. "Mr. Martin?" *Thank God.* Let's get this over with.

I follow the slim detective as he gimps down a hall of doors until we stop at a room on the left. *Interview room 3.* He gestures for me to enter.

"Would you like a bottle of water?" The detective asks, still lingering in the doorway.

"No, thank you. I'm fine." *I'm not fine.* I sit and cross my arms. It's freezing in here.

He comes in and shuts the door. "I'm sorry for your wait. I understand you've been here for a while. My name is Detective Parker. I'll be handling the investigation." He takes a seat and begins. "Mr. Martin, ..."

I hold up my hand. "Thomas, please."

"Alright. Thomas, can you tell me about your relationship with the victim?"

"Yes. Of course." I pause, feeling emotional. I steel myself. "We go way back. I went to law school with him. We were roommates for a couple of years back then." Memories flood my mind, and I push them back. "Currently, we are business partners. We own a law firm together." I dispatch a hefty sigh. "I guess we *did* own a law firm together."

"How have things been going with the business?"

"We've been going gangbusters. Our firm specializes in medical litigation. It's been our most profitable year so far. Since we started, each year has been better than the one before." I lean forward, resting my head in my hands. I have a lot to figure out now that Jake's gone. He had his faults, but he was a damn good lawyer and the real money-maker at our firm.

Parker takes a sip of his coffee. "And the two of you argued tonight?"

Someone saw us. "Yes, we did, but it was no big deal." A wave of nausea rolls over me. I run my fingers through my thinning hair. "We were arguing about Cindy. She is one of the paralegals at our office. Last Friday, she came to me and told me Jake was handsy with her and made inappropriate comments to her as well. Sexual comments." I wish I would have taken the water after all. My mouth feels like it's full of cotton balls.

Detective Parker consults his list. "Are we talking about Cindy Prescott, who attended the party tonight?"

"Yes, that's right." I think back, "Actually, I was surprised she showed up, considering what happened with Jake."

"And she was with her husband tonight? He references his notes again: "Greg?"

"Yes, she was." *Was it him? Greg? Did he kill Jake?*

"What did she tell you happened between them? How was Mr. Carter handsy?"

"She told me about an incident in the copy room. Cindy said

it turned physical. He attempted to grope her or something along those lines. She didn't go into a lot of detail. I could tell she was uncomfortable talking about it." Detective Parker waits for me to continue. "I confronted Jake about it at the party and told him he can't do that kind of thing. She could sue us for sexual harassment, for crying out loud! We could lose our practice!" I throw my hands in the air. "But, Jake believes he's God's gift to all women. It was unfathomable to him that any woman would rebuff his attentions." I rub my forehead with both hands. I have a serious headache budding. "I've always felt sorry for Kimber. I don't know how she has stayed with him all these years. I can't tell you how many affairs he's had, dozens upon dozens, and those are only the ones I'm aware of."

Parker redirects, getting me back on track. "How did the two of you leave it? The argument."

"He said he would leave her alone, gave me a slap on the back, and went back inside the house. To be honest, I was pretty angry about how cavalier he acted about the whole thing, but that was classic Jake." I reconsider using the words *pretty angry* to describe my feelings. "You know, angry isn't the right word. I was *frustrated* because he wasn't taking it seriously."

Parker nods. "You said he went back inside after the argument. So the argument was outside?"

"Yes. We were out on the patio."

"Was there anyone else on the patio besides the two of you?"

"No, we were alone." It hits me. That was the last conversation I would ever have with Jake. My emotions rise again.

The detective continues lobbing questions. "Okay, at any

time during the night, did you go upstairs?"

"I did once, yes, to use the restroom."

"And when was that? Approximately?"

I fill my cheeks with air and release it slowly. "I have no idea. It was toward the end of the night."

"So, it wasn't too long before the body was discovered."

"I guess it wasn't too long before." *Should I have lied about going upstairs?*

"Was anyone else upstairs at the same time you were?"

I turn my palms up. "Not that I know of. I didn't see anyone."

The detective grimaces and shifts in his seat. "Did you see anyone else go upstairs during the night?"

"No. I didn't."

"Did you notice anything out of the ordinary? Anything at all?

I go over the night again before responding. "No, it seemed like everyone was enjoying themselves. It was the same as every other party, except for the new group of people."

"Are you referring to Mr. Carter's soccer friends?"

"Yes."

The detective jots something down in his book. "Alright. Do you recall how much you had to drink?"

A lot, actually—four, maybe five Tom Collins. "A couple of Tom Collins, two, three at most."

"And how about your wife?"

"I wasn't paying attention. I would guess a few glasses of wine." I quickly add, "We didn't drive. We always take an Uber to their parties."

"I understand. Are you aware of any life insurance policies

Jake may have had?"

"He didn't share his personal finances with me. But he was the breadwinner for his family, and he would have wanted them to be taken care of. I'm sure there's a policy in Kimber's name." I pause. *This is going to sound like another motive.* "And there is a policy in the name of the practice."

Detective Parker's head pops up. "For how much?"

This isn't good. "The policy is for five million dollars." I rush to explain. "You must understand that Jake was a big draw for the firm. We were protecting the practice. You know, to help cover things while we recuperated in the event of his death." I add. "We have one on me too."

"And how much is the one on you?"

"Five hundred thousand," I say quietly. *Crap.*

Parker raises his eyebrows. "That's a substantial difference. Why?"

"I told you, Jake brought in the majority of our business. He has a reputation. Haven't you seen the commercials or the billboards? He was the face of our firm and a phenomenal lawyer." I shrug my shoulders. "We only did what made sense." Detective Parker looks skeptical. "I didn't do this, if that's what you're thinking. Five million sounds like a lot, but it's a drop in the bucket compared to what he would bring to the firm in the future."

Detective Parker taps his pen on the table and takes a moment. "Have there been any harassment issues involving Mr. Carter in the past?"

He's back to this. "There are no other *harassment* claims per se, but that doesn't mean he hasn't slept with most of the secretaries and aides over the years. He definitely has, but none of them have ever complained about it."

"So, you only confronted him this time because Mrs. Prescott formally complained?"

"Yes, I had no choice. Cindy is a sweet girl, but she could cause us some real trouble if she wanted to."

"Did you notice if her husband seemed agitated tonight?"

"No, I talked with him quite a bit, and he seemed like an intelligent, pleasant young man." I add, "I don't believe she told him about the sexual harassment thing with Jake, though."

"What makes you think that?"

"Well, I gave Cindy the week off with pay and use of my condo in Destin. It was a peace offering after what happened with Jake. Her husband seemed to think it was a bonus for good work."

"Instead of a buy-off?"

"A buy-off? Oh. No. I wouldn't call it that. There was never a discussion about any sort of deal. The trip and time off were my way of apologizing for Jake's behavior. That's all it was."

Detective Parker makes a note of something in his book. "Okay, Mr. Martin." He stands and offers me his hand and his card. "I appreciate your time. I'll be in touch. If anything else comes to mind, don't hesitate to call."

"Sure thing." I walk through the door and turn back to the detective, asking, "Could you speak to my wife next so we can get out of here?"

The detective nods, "Sure. I don't expect her interview to be any longer than yours."

"I appreciate it. Thank you."

DEVIL IN THE PITCH

CHAPTER TWENTY-ONE

Cindy Prescott
MNPD Criminal Investigations Division
Homicide Unit

Oh, Lordy. How can this be happening? Never in my wildest dreams did I believe I would be in a police station. But here I sit, still very drunk, mixed up in a murder investigation. One in which my very own husband might be the murderer! I should have stuck to my guns about not going to the party in the first place. If I had, maybe Mr. Carter would still be alive.

I'm in a terrible predicament. What in the world am I supposed to say when it's my turn to answer questions? I'll have to lie, of course, but I'll never be able to pull it off. Momma always told me the truth is in my eyes, no matter what's coming out of my mouth. I never got away with anything. *Oh, Greg, we're doomed.*

I can feel myself on the verge of a full-blown panic attack. *Breathe Cindy.* The room starts to spin. I close my eyes against the world and hope it will look different when I open them.

But staring at the inside of my eyelids only makes the spinning worse. *Dear Lord, please don't let me throw up in front of all these people.*

The far door creaks open. A likable-looking man in a blue button-down shirt tucked into khaki pants calls Mr. Martin's name. The man doesn't seem so scary. He's not at all what I expected. With any luck, he will ask me a few easy questions and let me be on my way. I guess that's the best I can hope for.

What I need are answers from Greg. I'm sure he can explain everything. It can't be as bad as it looks. *Can it?* I lean my head back against the wall and concentrate on my breathing. In my heart, I don't think Greg is capable of murder, but everything points in his direction.

Greg's *exact* words were, "I'm going to kill him." Of course, at the time, I never dreamed he actually meant it. Why would I? People say those words *all* the time. It's just an expression. I bet you've said it yourself. We *all* have.

But that isn't the only thing. Greg left to get another drink and then disappeared. He was gone for a good twenty minutes. He only showed up sweaty and panicked *after* the rest of us were already in the foyer. Where was he? What was he doing all that time?

Good Lady Alcohol burbles up, giving her opinion. "Obvi, Cindy, Greg was killing Mr. Carter. That's what he was doing. Duh!"

Be quiet! I put my head in my hands. Why did I have to drink so much wine?

The proverbial nail in Greg's coffin—the very worst thing—is that he lied. I can't explain why, but my honest, straight-laced husband *lied* to the police and then took off. Greg walked away and left me standing there with my mouth hanging open. He wouldn't have acted that way unless he was guilty of something. What other reason could there be?

After the murder, we all went to the living room. The room was silent aside from Mrs. Carter's sobbing. It wasn't long before the cops arrived, taking control of the scene and managing all of us. The whole ordeal was such a whirlwind. I didn't even have time to think.

Greg was thinking, though, wasn't he? That lie rolled right off his tongue. He told the officer he needed to pick up Ginny from the sitter because it was time for her medicine. Shame on him for that! Our Ginny is perfectly healthy, and everyone knows you don't lie about someone you love being sick or dying. It's bad karma. How could Greg do that?

"Umm ... Hello Cindy," says Lady A, coursing through my veins. "He was fleeing the scene of his crime, where he murdered a man for touching you. Don't be a Naive Nellie!"

A glimpse of my future flashes through my mind. It's a bleak picture. I see years of family portraits, all with Greg in orange, lining the mantel. Our sweet little girl will draw sun-shiny pictures for her daddy to hang on his cell wall. And I will have to make regular deposits to Greg's commissary account so he can buy Cheetos and canned chili. *Ugh!*

I get lost in a maze of conjecture, and before long, Mr. Martin comes back into the room and is exchanged for his wife. It hits me as I watch her walk away with the detective. *I could be next!*

My flight or fight response kicks in, and flight wins. *I need to get out of here.* Why didn't I think of this before? I'll tell the officer I need to use the restroom. Instead, I'll leave. I'll order a Lyft to take me home, and later blame my lapse of judgment on the drinking.

Lady A. responds with enthusiasm, "Now you're cooking, Girlie! That is an excellent idea!"

I stand as the door squeaks open. "Cindy Prescott?" A bearish man standing in the doorway barks out my name, his face in a frown. *Crap! Crap! Crap!*

It's not the same man who came for the Martins. This one is wearing a police uniform. *Oh, God! Does that mean something? Is he taking me straight to jail? Where is the nice-looking man in the khakis? Breathe, Cindy, breathe.* I raise my hand and say, "Here," as if my teacher had called my name for attendance.

The husky officer gestures with his bear paw for me to come while Lady A. needles again, "Well, here we go. You're toast now, sister!"

The man, whose eyes are like little black buttons, grunts, "Follow me." He doesn't seem friendly at all. I trail after him as he leads the way with his hand resting on his holster, at the ready.

We walk to the very end of the hall, and I'm pleased to see it isn't a jail cell. The sign on the door reads, Interrogation Room 4. "Wait in here," he grunts in a deep voice. "Detective Parker will be with you soon."

I take in the new environment. The room smells like old pennies, reminding me of Grandpa's vintage 1974 Pinto. It's dank in here, stale, like a musty basement, and it could use a fresh coat of paint. I trace a name carved on the table with my finger and imagine all the people who have sat in this chair before me. Real criminals were in this *same* chair, and now *I'm* the one sitting here. If I lie about anything during my interview, that makes me a criminal too. *Greg, what have you done?*

After a few minutes, it occurs to me that I'm in this room alone and unsupervised. I debate calling Greg. Can they arrest me for using my phone after they told me not to? I don't think they can. It's not like I was court-ordered not to use it. It was more of a suggestion than an request. *Right?*

Lady Alcohol hiccups and says, "Yep, Cindy, you got it. That is totally accurate."

As I pull out my cell phone, the man in khakis opens the door and walks through. My fingers release the phone, sending it to the bottom of my clutch with a clonk. My traitorous face flushes immediately.

"I'm Detective Parker. I understand it's been a long night ...." He stops mid-sentence and stares at me. "Can I get you a water or anything?"

"No thank you. I'm fine."

He looks doubtful. "Are you sure? It's no problem."

I consider explaining for the millionth time that my face turns into a hot, flaming cherry when I'm stressed. But I don't have the energy. "I'm good, but thank you."

"Okay." The detective takes a seat. "I only have a few questions for you, and then we will get you out of here." He flips to a clean page in his notebook. I see him write my name at the top and underline it. "I understand you worked for the victim."

I nod. "He was one of my bosses. I work as a paralegal for Carter & Martin. That's the firm's name." *I guess it will only be Martin now. I hope I don't lose my job. Especially if Greg goes to jail! Somebody has to buy the diapers.* I continue, "I haven't been working there long, only about four months."

"Have there been any problems since you started? Any complaints?"

Shoot. I know where this is going. So much for a few easy questions. He's already talked to Mr. Martin, meaning he most likely knows about the sexual harassment. I have no choice. "Yes, there have been some problems." Fiddling with the zipper on my clutch, I tell the detective what happened. "There was an issue with Mr. Carter. Early on, he made comments about my body—inappropriate, sexual comments."

Detective Parker waits for me to elaborate. When I don't, he nudges me along. "Such as?"

"Umm ... Mr. Carter said my rear end is smoking hot." I make air quotes when I say the words smoking hot. "Only Mr. Carter didn't say rear-end. He used a different word." The detective is still looking at me, waiting for another example.

I switch which leg is crossing the other. "There was another time. Mr. Carter called me a tease because he could see my ... nipples through my shirt." I *hate* talking about this. "He made a joke about keeping the thermostat down all the time. I started wearing a padded bra after that."

The detective continues, "At any point did it become physical?"

"Yes. I'm afraid it did."

"Can you tell me more about that?"

I take a deep breath. "I was in the copy room, and Mr. Carter came up behind me and pinned me against the copier. He ... ummm, pressed his ... pelvic area against my ... butt, and I could feel his ... well, he had ... an erection."

"Ha Ha Ha Ha Ha!" The wine chimes in. "Er, er, er ... erection!"

Detective Parker presses for more details. "Is that all that happened?"

Isn't that enough? I shake my head. "No. He slipped his hand underneath my arm and grabbed my ... breast. I told him I would scream, and I threw an elbow. He laughed like it was hilarious, but he did back off."

Detective Parker leans in. "When did this happen?"

"Last Friday."

"And you told this to Mr. Martin?"

"Yes, I told Mr. Martin after Mr. Carter left for the day."

"And what did Mr. Martin tell you?"

"Mr. Martin said he would be out of the office all this week and told me I could take it off too, with pay. He even offered his condo in Destin and said we could stay there for free. I imagine he was afraid I would sue the firm or something." I shrug. "Anyway, he told me he would take care of it," I added. "That's what they were arguing about at the party."

"You overheard what they were arguing about?"

"No, I was inside." As the words come out of my mouth, I realize my mistake.

The detective has realized it too. "If you didn't hear them, how do you know what they argued about?"

Dang it, Cindy! "I *assumed.* That was what I meant to say. You know. Because Mr. Martin said he would talk to him about it." I can tell the detective is trying to figure out if I misspoke or if I'm lying. My face is on fire. "Could I have some water now, please?"

I need a time-out from this little hole I dug for myself. Detective Parker gets up without saying anything and leaves to get the water. He returns and slides the bottle across the table.

"Thanks." I take my time unscrewing the cap and take a long, slow sip.

The questions resume. "Did you have any contact with Mr. Carter at the party?"

"Yes, not long after we arrived, he came up to us and said it was good to see me and nice to meet Greg." I take another sip of water. *Please, let me go home.*

"Was that your only interaction with him tonight?"

"Yes."

"Was your husband with you the whole time you were at the party?"

"He was, except for when he went outside for a smoke." *And when he went to get another drink, he disappeared for twenty minutes.*

"Did you see your husband go outside to smoke?"

"I didn't *watch* him go out the door, but I heard him ask Mrs. Carter if it was okay to go out on the patio and smoke. And when he came back, he smelled like smoke."

Detective Parker straightens out one of his legs. "What were you doing while your husband was outside?"

"Oh, I got something to eat. It was like a little meat pie."

"Were you drinking alcohol?"

Sure was. "Yes, I was drinking wine."

"How many glasses?"

Four. "Three. I know that's a lot, but I was nervous being there."

He nods. "I understand. Did you go upstairs at any point while you were at the Carter's house?"

"Upstairs? No."

"Did you see anyone else go up the stairs?"

I shake my head. "No."

"Were you angry enough about the harassment to want to harm Mr. Carter?"

"Of course not!" *I can't believe Greg put me in this situation, here alone, dealing with it all by myself.* "I don't know anything else, and it's late. I should get home to my little girl."

"Soon. I have a few more questions. Did you argue with your husband tonight while you were at the party?"

Someone saw us. "Oh," I say, taking another long sip. "I wouldn't call it an argument. Greg doesn't like when I drink too much. And, like I said, I had several glasses of wine with very little food. It wasn't a big deal. He thought I'd had enough. That's all." *I'm lying to a detective. I am now a criminal.* My heart is thumping in my chest.

"Is your husband aware of the harassment?"

Yes. "No, Greg doesn't know anything about it. I didn't think it was necessary to tell him. I went to Mr. Martin about it. I believed he would take care of it. He promised me he would."

"Was it your husband they released at the scene?"

"Mm-hmm. The officer let him go home to tend to our daughter. She's been sick." I hate hearing those words come out of my mouth, and softly knock on the underside of the table with my knuckles. I don't think it's real wood, but it's better than nothing.

The detective studies me. "Why were you late to the party?"

"As I'm sure you can understand, I didn't want to go to the party after what happened with Mr. Carter. But it has been marked on the calendar for two months, and my husband was looking forward to it. We argued about it. I didn't want to tell him why I didn't want to go, so I told him I had a headache. Then he got mad and started slamming things around. So, I gave in and agreed to go."

The detective appears to have had an ah-ha moment. "He was slamming things around. It sounds like he has a temper."

Oh my gosh, Cindy! "No, Greg isn't violent if that's what you're thinking. He was *irritated* because he didn't want to miss an opportunity to schmooze with big-time lawyers. Greg is all about networking."

"Were you afraid if you told your husband the truth, he would do more than slam cabinets? Is that why you didn't tell him?"

Dang it, Cindy, look what you've done! "No, nothing like that. I was worried that if he knew what happened with Mr. Carter, he would want me to quit, and it's a really, really good job. That's the only reason I didn't tell him. I have *never* been afraid of my husband. Greg isn't like that!"

Detective Parker writes a word I can't make out, followed by a question mark, in his notebook. "Tell me where you were at the time the body was discovered?"

Not with Greg. "I was with Greg in the living area. As I said, we were together all night except when he went out for a smoke. He wasn't outside long, and then we were together the rest of the night." I search the detective's eyes, wondering if he sees the lack of truth in mine.

"Is there anything else you can think of that might be important? Did you see anything unusual or out of the ordinary? Anything at all?"

"No, nothing." I smooth an imaginary wrinkle from my dress. "Nothing at all. I can't believe it happened." I take another swig. "I'm still processing it."

Detective Parker leans back in his chair and puffs some air out of his cheeks. After what seems like forever, he says, "Alright then, Mrs. Prescott. That's all for now." He stands and hands me his business card. "Thank you for your time. I'm going to get a patrol officer to take you home." He leads me out of the room. "I'll be in touch with your husband very soon. Tell him I still need to get his statement."

Not before we get our stories straight, you won't. "Yes, I'll be sure to tell him. Thank you, detective."

◆ ◆ ◆

I crawl into the back of the squad car for a second time, desperate to talk to Greg. There is no way I can ask him the questions I need to with an officer two feet away, but I need to hear his voice. Tell him I'm coming home. I hit *Hubby* from my call list. *Come on, Greg, pick up.* The phone goes straight to voicemail. I try again with the same result.

I shove the phone back in my clutch and run through possible scenarios. What if Greg skipped town and turned off his phone to avoid the police tracking him? Would he do that?

Would he leave Ginny and me for a life on the run?

As the officer pulls up in front of our apartment building, I see that our apartment window is dark. *That's worrisome.* If he was home, I know he would wait up for me. My eyes scan the lot for his car. Nothing. His car isn't here. *Greg. No.*

The officer opens my door. Still feeling nauseous, I step out of the cruiser with my shoes in my hand. I try to take another step, but my feet don't want to move forward. I'm not ready for my life to take such a turn. I want to hit the pause button right now. As I stand here now, a bright future is still a possibility. What happens after I walk through my front door might change everything.

Why isn't Greg's car here? If his car isn't here, then he isn't either. There is only one reason why he wouldn't be here, one reason for his disappearance at the party, and one reason why our light isn't on. He did it. My husband is a murderer on the run.

"Now, you don't know that, Cindy Jo," Momma says in my head. "You're jumping the gun, sugar. Give the boy a chance."

She's right. I don't know anything. I need to give Greg the benefit of the doubt.

I stand for a minute outside our apartment, building up my courage. I try the knob. It's unlocked. "Greg?" I drop my shoes on the ground. The lights are off, and it's super quiet. I flip on the light and move towards our bedroom. My heart sinks, finding it empty. It's the same with the kitchen and our bathroom.

My last hope rests on Ginny's closed door. *Please, please be in here.* I push the door open. *Thank God.* Here he is, rocking our baby in the same rocker my Nana rocked me in. Greg puts a finger up to his mouth. I watch as he slowly rises and lays Ginny in her crib. She stirs, but Greg pats her bottom, settling her right down. He's such a good daddy. It only makes me love him more. I move out of the doorway as he backs out and pulls the door closed.

We walk towards the living room. My words come tumbling out. "Oh my gosh, Greg. I've been so worried. They wouldn't let us use our phones at the police station." My eyes well up. "On my way home, I tried to call you, but it went straight to voicemail, and then I didn't see your car."

He snorts, "The lot was full. That guy with all the potted plants on his porch was having a party. I had to park in the side lot." He continues with a grimace. "My phone ... I dropped it when I was leaving the Carter's. The screen is toast. I could hear it ringing, but I couldn't answer it. I turned it off so I could get Ginny settled down. All she wanted was you." He puffs his cheeks. "I've been rocking her in there forever."

"It was all so terrible." A tear slides down my face. "I was so worried." He pulls me to him, and the tension in my body lets go. This man is my safe place, no matter what he's done. "We have a lot to talk about, Greg." I sit down on the couch. He sits beside me. "First, why would you lie about Ginny needing medicine? I can't believe you did that!"

He takes my hand. "I know, but I had to. I was so scared, Cin. I didn't know what else to do. I had to get away from there."

I'm almost scared to ask. "What were you afraid of?"

His eyes grow wide. "I thought I'd be next! I thought the killer might murder me too!"

I'm definitely missing something. "What? Why would

someone want to murder you? Tell me what happened."

"It was those damn goat cheese things at the party. I ate too many, I guess. You know my stomach. It was churning." He takes a ragged breath. "I watched Mr. Martin try the door of the bathroom downstairs. Somebody was using it. Then I saw him go upstairs."

He explains that after Mr. Martin came down, he went upstairs to use the bathroom. "I was in there awhile." He shakes his head. "I was in the middle of washing my hands when I heard the screaming. When I saw Mr. Carter at the bottom of the stairs, I panicked."

"I still don't understand, Greg. That doesn't make any sense. Why does where you went to the bathroom make a difference?"

He stares at me incredulously. "Because!" His voice sounds unusually high-pitched. "Cin, the murderer could think I saw something!" He takes a deep breath and ratchets it down a couple of notches. "Before I heard the screams, two sets of footsteps ran by the bathroom. They came from the front of the house, where the big stairs are, towards the back stairs, less than a minute apart. One of them had to have been the killer." He gasps. "Unless," he points his finger at me, "unless—they were working together."

"Two killers?"

"I don't know. I didn't *see* anything. I only heard the footsteps, but the killer or killers might not *know* that I didn't see anything. They could have seen me come down the stairs not too far behind them and *assumed* I saw something when I didn't."

He lowers his head. "I'm sorry I left you alone. It was a shit move, but I didn't know what to do."

I sigh with relief. "Oh my gosh, Greg, thank goodness!" I throw my arms around him. "I'm so relieved, I thought you were the murderer."

He pulls away. "Me? Seriously?" He looks genuinely hurt. "I can't believe you would think that about me."

I need him to understand. "You were the last person in the foyer. I had no idea where you were before that. And remember, you told me you wanted to *kill* Mr. Carter." I hurry to soothe his hurt feelings. "Those were your actual words, Greg. Not to mention, you lied to the police, and I didn't know why. Put yourself in my shoes! What would you have thought?" His expression softens. "When I couldn't get you on the phone, I thought you went on the run."

"Ha! Babe, I would never leave you and Ginny behind. We would have all gone on the run together." He pulls me in again.

I giggle and then remember how serious things still are. "You're going to have to talk to the detective tomorrow. Tell him everything you told me. You didn't actually see anything, so I don't think we have to worry about the killer or killers coming after you."

He nods. "So, tell me what happened to you."

"Most of it was just waiting for your turn to answer questions. We weren't allowed to talk or use our phones. So people were either staring at the walls or trying to sleep. The actual questioning was pretty quick, but I had to fudge a few things because I didn't know if I had to protect you."

"Fudge? What exactly did you have to fudge?" He looks at me as if he caught me stealing a candy bar or something.

Oh, dear. "Okay, but please remember, I was trying to *protect* you. I didn't know what you did or didn't do. So, when the detective asked if you knew about Mr. Carter and the harassment, I said no. I didn't want him to think you had a motive."

He sighs. "Anything else?"

"I went along with what you said about the sitter and Ginny. I don't think we have to admit lying about that." He nods, "And I said we were together when Mrs. Carter found the body." He wrinkles his nose. I let a few seconds pass. "Also, I guess someone saw us arguing. The detective asked what we were arguing about, and I said you were mad at me for drinking too much."

"Cindy! That makes it seem like I'm trying to control you! Like I'm an abusive husband or something!"

I put my hand on his knee. "There's one more thing, and it's a little worse."

The color drains from his face. "Worse? How is it worse?"

Ugh. I don't want to tell Greg this part. "I also told him we were late to the party because I didn't want to come and that I only agreed after you slammed the cabinets and stuff."

"Cindy!" His voice rings high again. "What were you thinking?"

"Well, Greg, I did the best I could. You left me all alone. I had no idea where you were or what you did. I needed to make up something quick about the fight because people saw us. And I had to tell him why we were late because he flat-out asked me." I shrug and shake my head. "I was still drunk, you know. And I'm a terrible liar! You can't be mad at me for that."

"I'm not *mad*, but this changes everything." He shakes his head. "I don't think we can tell the detective the truth." I see the anxiety all over his face. He's rattled. "I *do* have a motive. And I *was* upstairs when it happened. That's not good. That's not good at all!" He pauses. "Plus, what if other people noticed that I was the last one in the foyer? All those things, on top of the things you told the detective, I'm going to look guilty as hell."

"I've never seen him this stressed. It scares me. "Let's get some sleep, babe. We can talk about it when we're fresh in the morning. I'm so tired I can't even think straight."

"How am I supposed to sleep?" He puts his head in his hands. "Cin, the murderer was one of us from the party. If I tell the truth, it will give them all the ammunition they need to put me at the top of the list. Motive. Means. Opportunity. It's all there, and it all points directly to me!"

"I don't know, Greg. If you get caught lying, it'll be even worse."

"But *you* lied! It is already bad! Sometimes, cops get tunnel vision. Innocent people are convicted all the time, Cin! It's too risky."

I stand and tug on his hand. "Come on. Let's at least lie down." I won't say so, but he has a point. I'm his wife. I know him better than anyone, and I thought he'd done it. Greg is right. Lying might be our only hope.

CHAPTER TWENTY-TWO

Detective Parker
The Morning After the Murder

After five restless hours of sleep, I drag myself back into the office. Someone has placed a newspaper on my desk. The headline screams at me: PROMINENT LOCAL ATTORNEY MURDERED IN HIS OWN HOME. Great. It's not like I didn't expect the media to pick this up. I knew this would be a high-profile case from the get-go, but I thought I'd have a little more time. I had never heard of the guy before, but it seems he was some kind of local celebrity. In a city with so many famous residents, that's saying something.

After grabbing a coffee, the first of many today, I call Maddie. "Tell me something good, Maddie."

Maddie groans, "I don't have much, Sol. I'm sorry to say. The powder turned out to be cocaine, as you suspected. We found a baggie with a small amount of it inside the desk. It's minimal, though. We also found a box of marijuana in the lower right desk drawer; the one you noted was ajar. It's way over the felony limit, 7.2 ounces."

The law in Tennessee, at least for now, considers anything exceeding .5 ounces to be a felony. But I'm not about to jam up Mrs. Carter over some weed. In our neighboring Kentucky, anything under 8 ounces is a misdemeanor. Both items were found in the victim's office, so as far as I'm concerned, they were his.

"What about the knife?" I ask.

"The knife was a total bust. The killer must have used gloves and cleaned the knife prior. There were no prints at all. No partials. Nothing. We sent it for DNA, but I bet the only DNA to show up will be the victim's." She continues, "Tech is going through the laptops now. So far, all they've found is some run-of-the-mill porn on both the victim's computer and the son's. They haven't gotten to the phones yet."

I was hopeful about the knife. "What about video?"

"We pulled the footage from the security camera in the backyard. It's ready to view. Also, the uniforms found a camera directly across the street. It has a clear view of the Carter's front door, but I'm afraid that's all I've got for you."

It's not much to go on. "Thanks, Maddie." I hang up the phone and call the M.E. "Hey Judy, do you have anything on Jake Carter yet?"

"Yeah, I was going to send the report to your email. It's pretty straightforward; sending it now."

"Great, thanks." A moment later, a ding confirms an incoming email. I skim through the report.

Well-developed male. 44 years old. 6 ft. 4 in. tall and 237 lbs. Stab wound to the upper torso. Depth of penetration: 8 ½ inches.

Cause of death: Penetrating trauma to the ascending aorta secondary to a cervical fracture of C2.

Manner of death: Homicide.

The toxicology report shows his alcohol level was 0.10 %. His blood was positive for cocaine but no marijuana or other drugs. I have to hope something will pop up on his laptop or phone.

I look up the number for Greg Prescott. It goes straight to voicemail. I do the same with Molly and George Powell. Neither one answer, and both voicemail boxes are full.

Frustrated, I pull out my notebook. Every interview is videotaped, but I like to jot things down. Flipping to the right page, I read over the entries I made last night.

Kimber Carter
Wife
Admits drinking a lot
States vic had an affair with sister-in-law 4yrs prior
Denies ever having her own affair
Saw an argument between office aide Cindy and her husband, Greg
Talking to Angela prior to finding VIC
Life insurance?

Lizzy Santos
Arrives early 6 p.m.
Neighbor for 10 yrs.
Witnessed Thomas Martin, the business partner, arguing with

the victim

   Saw Collin Montgomery go upstairs

   In the kitchen with Eli Carter for at least 15 minutes before the body was found

   Specifically remembers, herself, Eli and Allie Carter, and Beth and Collin Mongomery in the foyer just after the body was found

   Still drunk??

<u>Eli Carter</u>

Younger brother

Still angry about the affair

Arrived approx. 8 p.m.

Confirms talking to the neighbor in the kitchen when the body was found

   and wife directly before that

   Lying about something!!!

<u>Allie Carter</u>

Acknowledges the affair with the victim

Told her husband about it that same day

Confirms her husband was with her until going into the kitchen to get a drink

<u>Beth Montgomery</u>

Has known victim for twenty years

Arrived around 6:30

Knew about the vic's previous affair. Claims she doesn't know

who it was with
  Vic's wife told her she thought he was having an affair currently
  Denies knowing anything about the wife having any affairs
  First time the soccer players attended one of the parties
  Believable

<u>*Collin Montgomery*</u>
A long-time friend of the couple
Denies ever going upstairs

<u>*Thomas Martin*</u>
Admits argument with victim over work-related sexual harassment
Claims vic had many affairs
Went upstairs to use the restroom. Saw no one else up there
Motive? Life insurance ??

<u>*Caitlin Martin*</u>
Unaware of the harassment issue or anything else related to business
Nothing here

<u>*Cindy Prescott*</u>
Confirms sexual harassment. Claims husband is unaware
Saw Martin and Carter fighting
Confirms the argument with her husband. Claims it was over her drinking

Husband violent?
Lying??

<u>Dan Agee</u>
Soccer teammate
Known vic less than six months
Admitted to doing a line of coke with the victim no more than twenty minutes before he was found dead

The timeline is everything. If Agee is telling the truth, that leaves a very narrow window for the murder to occur. I keep reading the rest of the notes. The remainder of the soccer group, including my friend Julian, added very little.

They all had the same story. They were all together, as a group, in the living room the entire time, except for drinks, food, or bathroom breaks. They all denied going upstairs. Several said Mrs. Carter was with them in the living room the hour prior to finding the body.

I log into my computer to do a little research on life insurance policies. It's not uncommon for a partner in a business to be insured. After taking a gander at the company's financials, I'm not sure the five million will be enough. Jake was the face of the law firm. He brought in the majority of the business. His death hurts Thomas Martin far more than it would help him.

As for Kimber Carter, the life insurance is substantial. They own three separate policies with a combined total of twenty million dollars. And that's only the life insurance. There is over four hundred thousand in the joint checking account. And tons of money in various investments.

Money is a common motivator for murder, for sure. But she is alibied by multiple witnesses as having been in the living room the hour prior. She could have enlisted one of the partygoers to do it, but my gut tells me this was about something else entirely.

The victim's brother has a hell of a motive, but why wait four years to do something about it? Besides, Lizzy Santos said she was with him in the kitchen when the body was found. And that they were talking for at least fifteen minutes. He would have to kill his brother and, within minutes, carry on a normal conversation with the Santos woman. I find it hard to believe. I'm still convinced the killer was upstairs when Mrs. Carter found her husband.

My phone rings, and I answer, "Parker."

"Hello, Detective Parker. This is Greg Prescott. My wife said you wanted to speak about the party last night."

He called me. "Yes, thank you for calling. Could you come to the CID and talk to me this morning?"

"Sure, I can be there in an hour."

"Sounds good! I'll see you soon. Follow the signs to the Criminal Investigations Division." *I have a feeling about this guy.*

I head to the AV room to check out the videos and queue up the one pulled from across the street. Mrs. Carter comes home from her errands around 4:15 p.m. The house is quiet until 5:46 p.m. when a woman exits the side gate. Based on Kimber Carter's statement, I believe it to be the maid.

I see Lizzy Santos walk from her house to the Carter's about ten minutes later. Followed shortly by the caterers. Seventeen more people come onto the property after that. And aside from the caterer's departure, no one leaves the house before the police car arrives at 9:56 p.m.

Hoping for something better, I review the footage of the patio. I see the group of five sitting outside before the party begins. Everyone looks relaxed. They weren't out very long, and everything appeared normal.

There's nothing for some time. Then, I see Mrs. Carter talking with Collin Montgomery. I watch closely. They are only outside for a few minutes, but their body language with each other looks intimate. She touches his face and then takes his hand. Hmmm. *That's interesting*.

Next, a young man comes into view. Greg Prescott, I presume. He lights a cigarette and disappears behind the bar. Two and a half minutes later, Martin and Carter come outside. Martin is upset; it's obvious. Carter appears completely unfazed. He isn't bothered by Martin's railing in the least. Even through the video screen, I can feel Carter's condescending attitude.

Less than a minute after they return inside, Prescott reappears headed back into the house. He's walking in much faster than he did walking out.

Bingo! Prescott overheard the argument between Carter and Martin about his wife. There's a motive! He doesn't look like a match for Jake Carter, but if he ambushed him at the top of the stairs, that fits into my theory.

I'll have to see what comes from his interview, but I feel good about it. I check my watch. He'll be here any minute.

# DEVIL IN THE PITCH

CHAPTER TWENTY-THREE

Greg Prescott
MNPD Criminal Investigations Unit
Morning After the Murder

Cindy and I had a long discussion this morning about how this whole thing would play out. And we decided the truth was not our best option. If my own wife thought I was guilty, then there is a good chance a jury would too. That doesn't mean I'm not nervous about the interview. I will have to be on my game and keep my cool.

Talking to the police goes against everything I've learned in law school. I should refuse to speak to them without my attorney present, period. That's criminal defense class 101, but in this case, I feel it would make the situation worse.

So, we're rolling the dice and hoping it all works out. I'm not getting railroaded for something I didn't do. If things get hairy during the interview, I will invoke my right to an attorney. But I'm hoping it doesn't come to that.

The elevator dings as I arrive on the appropriate floor for the CID. I have to keep my wits about me. If this detective catches me in a lie, the outcome could be disastrous. I need to be two steps ahead of him and confident in my answers without coming off like an asshole.

Finding the waiting room, I take a seat, pull out my temporary burner phone, and text Cindy as planned:

Me: Hey, Babe. Just got downtown. I shouldn't be long. Do you need anything from the store?
Cindy: Yeah, we're low on peanut butter and chocolate milk. Thanks, Babe! Love you!
Me: Love you too! (kissy face emoji)

The idea is to show that I am not concerned about the interview. And that Cindy and I are good. You know, in case they ask for my phone.

I hit send, and a door opens.

"Mr. Prescott." A haggard-looking Detective Parker calls my name.

Walking towards him, I lead with my hand. "Nice to meet you." We shake. He has a firm handshake, which I try to match.

"Nice to meet you too. Follow me." He leads me to a small interview room.

The room is as expected. It's a tiny, cold room where the detectives have you sit in the corner, feeling trapped. It's all part of a psychological game to throw you off. It's not going to work on me, though.

In school, we studied police interviews and learned about nonverbal communication. AKA body language. While interviewing, detectives watch for indicators of deception:

dry mouth, licking the lips, profuse perspiration, excessive swallowing, and fidgeting. I have to keep my body relaxed and maintain eye contact. I take a seat and put on my game face.

Parker begins, "Thanks for coming in. Can I get you water or a coffee?"

"No thanks."

"Alright, as you know, I talked to your wife last night. It's my understanding she worked for the victim."

"Yes, for a few months now."

"How does your wife like the job?"

"She loves the work, and the pay is good."

"Was last night the first time you met either Mr. Carter or Mr. Martin?"

"Yes."

Parker shifts in his seat. "Your wife told me the two of you argued at the party. Can you tell me what you were arguing about?"

Her boss wanted to screw her. That's what it was about. I shake my head. "I don't like it when she drinks too much. We have a two-year-old to go home to. We can't go home drunk. I'm sure you can understand where I'm coming from."

Parker's face is deadpan. "We have some security footage that shows you on the patio during an argument between Mr. Martin and Mr. Carter. They were arguing about a sexual harassment issue at work."

Shit. Shit. Shit. Think! "Umm," *breathe*, "I did go outside to smoke a cigarette, but I didn't see anyone else out there. When I smoke, I like to listen to music. So I had my earbuds in the whole time." *Okay, nice recovery.* "I was leaning against the back of the bar, so I guess someone could have been out of my view, but I couldn't say." I flash my pearly whites. "But, as far as me hearing anyone, I had the music cranked. I wouldn't have heard a thing." *Ball's in your court, detective.*

"So you're telling me you don't know anything about a complaint your wife made to Mr. Martin about Mr. Carter?"

"Not until she came home from here last night. She told me the whole thing." I try to portray the right amount of dismay. I turn my hands up. "I was shocked, but she said she wanted to handle it herself." I keep it rolling. "I'm so proud of her for reporting him and standing up for herself!" *Man, I'm killing it!*

Detective Parker eyeballs me for a good five seconds. "I see." He finally says evenly. "Where were you when the body was discovered?"

Exactly as she told you. "I was with my wife in the living room area."

He keeps trying. "Why were you the one to go home to get your daughter instead of your wife?"

"Well, because Cindy had too much to drink. I couldn't let her drive." *Set and match.*

He narrows his eyes. "Right." He pauses. "Why were you late to the party?" He leans forward in his chair to make me feel even more boxed in.

I counter and lean toward him. "Cindy said she had a headache. I pushed her to go. Honestly, I was a bit of an ass about it." I lean back again; my body relaxed.

"Why was it so important for you to go?"

"I thought it would be a great networking opportunity. You know, rub elbows with some big-time lawyers." I smile like someone is taking my picture. I can see how annoyed he's getting, and I'm kind of digging it.

Parker makes some notes in his book and throws me another question. "Did you go upstairs at any time during the night?"

Yep. I sure did. "No. I didn't."

Parker asks, "If somebody told me they saw you go upstairs, what would you say?"

I'm trying to gauge if he's telling the truth or bluffing. My answer has to be the same either way: "I would say they were mistaken. I never went upstairs."

He leans back in his chair, defeated. "Can you think of anything else that could be helpful to this investigation?"

"No, nothing. I wish I could help." *Home free!*

Reluctantly, Parker stands up and offers his hand. "Okay, Mr. Prescott, that's all I have for now."

CHAPTER TWENTY-FOUR

Eli

Night of the Murder

I watch as my brother tumbles head over feet down the stairs. I hear several cracks and then a sickening thud as he lands. I can't move. I'm not even breathing. Did this really happen?

I realize I have to make a quick decision. There's no time for second-guessing. I step over my brother's crooked body and run up the stairs, across the hall, and then down the back stairs. I've made the decision, and I am prepared to live with it.

For the record, I do know what happened between Jake and Allie. But I didn't hear it from Allie. Jake is the one who told me. He called me right after it happened.

The details of that day are scorched into my memory forever. It was a Wednesday afternoon. The windows were open, and a light breeze wafted through the curtains. I was washing the mushrooms for dinner. We were having chicken marsala. Allie would be home by six. She told me she had errands to run after work. There was a bottle of red wine breathing on the counter. I remember Joe Cocker was playing on the radio when the phone rang.

Jake's voice crowed on the other end, "I just fucked your wife, little brother." A wave of nausea bubbled up from somewhere deep inside. I knew he wasn't lying. He would never say anything he couldn't back up. "She's on her way home to you right now." He continued, sticking the knife in a little deeper. "You should let her shower before you take a turn with her. But take it easy on her, Bro. I hit it pretty hard." He laughed, "Thanks for sharing." He disconnected the call, and I vomited over the colander full of freshly washed mushrooms.

It is a twenty-minute drive from Jake's house to mine. Those were the longest twenty minutes of my life. As I sat on the couch waiting for my wife to come home, Jake's words pinged around in my mind—fucked your wife, hit it hard, thanks for sharing.

Finally, I heard her tires crunching the gravel as she pulled up to the house, and then the sound of the engine turning off. I waited to hear the car door close, but I heard nothing. I wondered if she would come back to me at all. When she finally walked through the door, tears rolled down her face.

"Allie." It was all I could get out. She looked so small and vulnerable to me.

"Eli, I have to tell you something. I'm so sorry. I'm so, so sorry, but I...."

I interrupted her. I didn't want to hear it coming from her mouth. I pushed out my hand. "Allie, I know. Jake called. Please don't say anything right now. I need to digest it. We can talk about it after you shower." I hated asking her to do *exactly* what

Jake suggested, but I needed her to wash him off. I tried to push back images of Jake all over her, inside of her, but of course, that is an impossible thing to do.

She left me alone with my thoughts and went to do as I asked. I needed to figure this out. We belonged together. Allie was everything I ever wanted. She still is. I know better than anyone how Jake can worm his way into people's lives, and into their minds. He's a master manipulator who knows how to get what he wants.

Of course, I know Jake didn't do this all by himself. Allie wasn't innocent in what happened. I know that. But I decided to forgive her, and with that, I understood I had to forgive her completely, with my whole heart. I couldn't hold on to even one tiny grain of bitterness toward her. If I did, it would only fester and destroy everything we'd built together. I couldn't let Jake take it all away from me.

Allie and I decided together not to tell Kimber about the phone call. She didn't need to know that her husband called me to brag about what happened.

We let a whole year pass by before going back to their house. But Allie and I love Kimber and the kids. We want to be a part of their lives. If I had let Jake take them away from me, then he would have won. I decided he didn't get to win anymore.

Having sex with Allie was by far the worst thing he has ever done to me, but he's been torturing me for a very long time. On my first day of elementary school. Jake, a fourth-grader that year, offered to show me around. He roped an arm around my shoulder as he pointed out the lunch room, the media center, and the big kids' playground.

To this day, I still remember the clothes I was wearing. Everything was new: jeans, a white collared shirt, and Ninja Turtle tennis shoes. My mom and I picked them out together the day before.

My big brother said, "Let me show you where the bathroom is, so you'll know." He led me into the boy's room. Once the door closed, he pushed me into the corner. At first, I thought he was goofing around. But he started undoing his pants. A few seconds later, I felt the warmth of urine. Jake was peeing on me. He peed on my crotch and down my legs. When he was done, Jake pointed at me and laughed, holding his belly. He laughed so hard.

Jake opened the bathroom door. "You pissed your pants, little brother!" He hooted. He made sure to say it loud enough for the kids in the hall to hear. I looked down at my new pants and shoes, now soaked in Jake's urine, and knew I had to walk out of the bathroom into a hall full of kids looking like I had peed myself. I was only five years old.

The kids teased me mercilessly after that. The entire student body started calling me PEE-li. I became the runt of the litter, the weakling, the one all the other pups ganged up on. Even worse, my parents didn't believe me when I told them what happened. Jake swore up and down that he didn't do it. He said he would *never* do something so horrible, and they believed him. They punished me for lying about it and not taking responsibility for my *accident*.

That wasn't an isolated incident, either. Jake made my life miserable whenever he could. If I had something, he took it. If I built something, he tore it down.

Do you want to know the worst part? Jake really was better than me at everything. My brother was a better athlete, a better student, and he got accepted to a better college. Every girl I ever liked, liked him better. For me, that was the real kick in the teeth. How is it fair that he could be so evil and then be so blessed? Why did he get to be King Midas? I have struggled with that question all my life.

When I return to the kitchen, Lizzy is the only one there. She is sitting in the same place she has been all night. All the others are congregating in small groups in the living room. I grab a glass and pour myself some whiskey. I wonder if she can see my hands shaking. She asks me a question about the crab croquettes. I throw back the rest of my drink and wait.

It's only a few minutes before we hear screaming from the foyer. *Kimber has found him.* We all crowd behind her. Collin steps up and turns her away from Jake's body. The weight of what happened hits me. Jake is dead. He will never hurt me again.

◆ ◆ ◆

Fifteen Minutes Earlier

I'm standing with Allie as she talks to Beth. Beth is talking about her kids and all the activities they're into. I've watched those kids grow up at countless pool parties and bar-b-ques. I've even coached a few of their teams over the years. They call me Uncle Eli. I love them like family.

I excuse myself from the group with the story that I'm going to get a drink, but instead, I steer toward Jake's office. There's only one good thing about my brother: He always has the best weed. At every party, I raid the stash he keeps in his office. It helps me wind down in the evenings and relax.

Plopping myself into Jake's office chair, I pull the wooden box out of the bottom right desk drawer. When I open the lid, I find the box full. *Cool.* I take a baggy out of my pocket and cop enough to roll a few blunts.

I'm returning the box to the drawer when I notice Lizzy standing at the top of the stairs. She looks so strange. Something weird is going on. She doesn't see me in here; the room is dark, and I never turned on the lights. I keep watching and see Jake waltzing into the foyer, heading straight for the stairs. *He knew she would be there*. She is waiting for him. *No.* Are they having an affair? Lizzy always seemed immune to Jake's bravado. I can't believe it.

I watch Jake jog up the stairs, and as he reaches the last step, Lizzy pulls a large knife from behind her back. In one fluid motion, she brings the knife over her head and into Jake with such force that I lose my breath.

Jake falls backward down the stairs. My mouth hangs open as I look at Lizzy and then back at Jake. She removes a pair of blue latex gloves, shoves them into her pocket, then turns on her heels and heads toward the back stairs.

It takes a beat for me to process what's happened. Jake is dead. Lizzy murdered him. My mind runs through my next steps. I can't come back into the living room through the foyer. If someone sees me, I would have to either claim to be guilty or tell them what I saw, and I don't want to do either.

I dart across the foyer, stepping over my brother's body. I run through the upstairs hall and down the back staircase. No one is in the kitchen but Lizzy. She is sitting quietly on her stool, cool as a cucumber. I grab a new glass and pour a little whiskey, my hand shaking.

Lizzy is eyeing me, trying to figure out if I saw anything. She says, "Did you have any of the croquettes? You really should have. They are delicious." Something happens between us. We come to some sort of unspoken agreement. We are now each other's alibi. I will never tell anyone what I saw, not even Allie. Whatever he did, I know Jake deserved it.

CHAPTER TWENTY-FIVE

Lizzy

Two Days Before the Party

Today is Wednesday, and that means laundry. I dump an armload of warm clothes on the bed with a grunt. The smell of clean laundry always makes me feel like all the air in my house is fresh. Which, of course, it isn't. I'm a barely-keeping-my-head-above-water kind of cleaner. Dusting is never at the top of my to-do list. Most of the time, it's not on the list at all. So, the air in my house is full of cat hair and dust motes. You can see them dancing in the air wherever the sun shines through the windows.

As I'm folding, I glance out the window and have to do a double-take. I can't possibly have seen what I think I have. I look again. Sure enough, I see Jake and Kimber having sex in their laundry room. *Holy Shit!* I've caught them *in flagrante delicto!* Oh, this is spicy! I know I shouldn't watch, but I move closer to the window anyway. *Wait a minute.* That's not Kimber!

The woman is folded over the washing machine, her hand pressed against the window, her chestnut-brown hair hiding her face. Jake stands behind her, wearing a white t-shirt. But this woman isn't wearing a stitch. His hands are on her hips, his pelvis driving against her hard, almost violently. The woman's breasts surge forward with every thrust.

I can't believe this! Jake has some nerve to have sex with another woman in the house he shares with his wife. *Poor Kimber.* What a lech he is! He never fooled me with his phony charm. I always knew he was a snake in the grass!

I pull the drapes closed with enough of a slit to keep peeking without being seen. *Who knew I was such a voyeur?* I watch as the woman tosses back her hair. She has a broad smile on her face. She is loving it. She looks so familiar to me. I hone in on her face. Oh my God! That's not a woman. That's my Chloe!

Dizzy, I have to sit down on the bed. My mind is racing. What should I do? Should I run over there right now? *No.* I remember the expression on Chloe's face. She was enjoying it. Jake wasn't forcing her to do anything.

How could Jake even see her that way? He has watched Chloe grow up. She was only seven years old when we moved here, for Christ's sake! Her birthday parties have been at their pool since she was ten! I feel like I'm going to pass out. My fingers rub at my eyes in a futile attempt to extract the image from them. Could I have imagined it? *No, definitely not.* I know what I saw. I saw Jake Carter fucking my daughter.

Oh my God! The realization hits me like a ton of bricks. Jake is the boyfriend Chloe has been on cloud nine about. Bile rises in my throat. Should I go to Kimber? Should I call John and tell him he needs to come home immediately? *Take a breath, Lizzy.* I have to calm down so I can think. I need to find out more information before I do anything. *I wonder if she still keeps a diary.*

I check the clock. It's 2:10. Chloe said she would be home by

2:30. Her friend Melanie is picking her up around 3:00. After she leaves, I'll look for her diary. I peek out the window again. *Thank God*. This time, the window is empty.

I sit in the living room waiting for my child, hoping that a search of her face will give me some clue as to where her head is. Could I have misread her face in the window? Maybe she wasn't enjoying it. Maybe Jake forced her somehow. *Maybe, maybe, maybe. Maybe, I'm in denial.* I know what I saw. It happened; she wanted it, and now I have to do something about it.

My front door opens, and Chloe bounces through, beaming from ear to ear. She is glowing. To be honest, it's hard to look at her. All I see is her hand pressed against the window, but I can't let on that I know until I figure out what I'm going to do.

"Hey, sweetie." I try to sound normal, but my voice cracks. "Did you have a nice swim?"

"It was great," she says with sickening enthusiasm. Her face gives nothing away. No one would ever know she was having sex with a forty-four-year-old man, my best friend's husband, fifteen minutes ago. She bops right by me. "I'm going to go get in the shower." With that, Chloe springs up the stairs. I can only sit there with my head spinning, unable to say anything else.

A half-hour and a half bottle of wine down my throat later, Chloe flits back downstairs. I'm shocked by her demeanor. This girl doesn't understand the dangerous game she is playing. Somewhere along the line, I failed her.

"Change of plans, Mom," she says, "I talked to Melanie, and we are going to the later movie instead. And then, if it's okay, I'll spend the night at her house. Tomorrow we're going to the mall."

Drat. As chipper as my body allows, I respond. "Of course, that sounds like fun." I am chomping at the bit to search Chloe's room, but I am glad she is spending the night out. The more space between her and Jake, the better.

My mind is still roiling. How did it start? What did he say to entice her? How long has he been looking at her as a potential sexual partner? Last year? Two years ago? Three? A million scenarios go through my head, all of them horrible. Each is worse than the one before.

Chloe turns the TV on and flips through the channels, deciding on Law and Order SVU. We get through two episodes together, mostly in silence. I don't have any idea what to say. After the second episode, she turns to me. "What's for dinner? I'm starving."

I can't say anything. All I can do is stare at my child's beautiful face, lost in thought. My mind is filing through all the snippets of Chloe's life—her first steps, the first day of kindergarten, her eighth-grade graduation, and now the image of her having sex with Jake Carter. The memory of that is now lodged, along with the others, forever.

"Hello, Earth to Mom." Chloe is looking at me as though I have two heads.

"Oh, Umm...." I'm completely numb. "There is chili in the crockpot. You can help yourself. It's ready." Chloe disappears into the kitchen. I hear the sounds of her getting dinner. The silverware drawer opens and shuts, her bowl clangs on the counter, and I hear the sound of her humming. *She's humming!* She seems so happy. How can this be? Does she think that Jake would leave Kimber for her? Is that what he's told her?

I stand up and go to watch Chloe from the doorway. I wasn't planning to say anything. But the words slip out anyway. "So, when do I get to meet this boyfriend of yours?"

"Oh, I don't know. He's super busy with school and stuff." She turns to me. "Do we have any oyster crackers?"

"In the pantry."

She retrieves the crackers and sits down at the kitchen table.

I push. "It feels like I should have met him by now. It's your first real boyfriend. I would like to know more about him."

"Mom, stop. You'll meet him at some point. Why are you making such a big deal about it?" She delivers a spoonful of chili to her mouth and stares at me, staring back at her. "Can you let me eat, please? Jeez, Mom. You're acting so weird."

Tears bite my eyes. Don't cry, Lizzy. Not here. I leave the kitchen and climb up the stairs, feeling lost. How could this happen—my Chloe having a sexual relationship with Jake Carter? I shake my head. No! I will not accept this. This will end. He will never touch my girl again. I only have to figure out how to make that happen.

I splash cold water on my face and look in the mirror. The woman I see looks terrified. Why wouldn't she? Her baby girl has a cobra by the tail.

Chloe yells to me upstairs. "See you tomorrow, Mom. Love you!"

"Love you too, sweetheart!" I run to the window and watch the girls back out of the driveway. As soon as they're out of sight, I'm in Chloe's room. I start by looking between her mattresses. Nothing. Next stop, underwear drawer. I push the bras and panties out of the way. Bingo! Here it is, her diary. *That was easy.*

My fingers fumble to open it. Flipping through the pages, I find the last entry, and all the air escapes from my balloon. Chloe wrote this entry three years ago. *Ugh.* I skim through the pages, searching for Jake's name or anything sexual. Jake doesn't appear anywhere. The most scandalous entry talks about a boy named Bobby getting to second base.

A clue has to be here somewhere. I search the rest of Chloe's drawers and through her closet. I peek under the bed, finding an empty pizza box, but that's it. There must be something here somewhere.

Standing with my hands on my hips in the middle of the room, I look with fresh eyes. As I'm scanning, I see Chloe's day planner on her desk. Maybe I can glean some information from that. It's open to today's date. Written in Chloe's curly-q handwriting, I see a J within a circle and a bunch of hearts. I turn back the pages, horrified to see J after J going back over four months! I can't believe this has been happening next door, right under my nose.

I consider my options. Chloe is seventeen. Of course, I could go to the police. It's statutory rape. He might serve some time, but Jake is a big-shot attorney. I'm sure he would find a way around it. He could easily bribe a judge.

Besides, Chloe obviously thinks she is in love with him. She would hate me for reporting it. I know she would. We can all remember that young, desperate kind of love. The sort of love that, when you are in the throes of it, nothing else in the world matters. She would never forgive me. I would always be the villain who kept her from the love of her life.

Still, I have to stop this. Chloe's whole future is on the line. Jake needs to disappear. That's what needs to happen. The gears start spinning. If he turns up dead, I will be right by her side to console her. She will tell me her boyfriend dumped her or something along those lines to explain all the crying. And she will be okay. *We* will be okay.

The possibilities run through my mind. My brain goes straight to hiring a hitman, but where do you find one of those, and how much would it cost? A king's ransom, I imagine. Plus, it's risky to involve a third party. I'm going to have to do it myself.

I could poison him. I could sneak into the house and replace his sports drink with antifreeze. I've seen plenty of true crime shows about poisoning, but it can take a long time to work. And how would I ensure that Kimber or the kids didn't drink one? Poisoning is out.

Pacing back and forth in Chloe's room, I stop and look around. Heart and flower stickers are all over the back of her door. Her stuffed animals are piled one on top of the other in the corner. There are fairy lights strung across her headboard, for God's sake. She is so out of her depth with Jake. I have to figure this out.

Whatever method I choose, the most important thing is to leave no evidence behind. Nothing can lead the police back to me. That rules out firearms. The police can trace a gun. *Think, Lizzy.*

A light bulb goes off in my head. I remember that the Carters are having a party in two days. Kimber said that Jake invited some of his soccer friends and their wives. The more potential suspects, the better. Plus, alcohol flows like the Niagra at Carter parties. That's perfect. People will be laughing and drinking. No one will be paying attention to me or what I'm doing.

Okay! A plan is taking shape. Now I know when and where. I only have to figure out how. Jake is much too big for me to overtake physically, so strangling, suffocating, and bludgeoning are out. So is drowning, and I can't even imagine an electrocution scenario.

Stabbing? That could work, but Jake can't see me coming. I'll have to stab him in the back, or I don't stand a chance. And I'll only have one crack at it. That means I have to commit to it. I can use a knife from their knife block, and I'll have to wear gloves so I won't leave any fingerprints behind.

Can I pull this off? Yes—Yes, I can.

◆ ◆ ◆

One day before the Party

I pull in front of a little boutique in Franklin's charming downtown. I'm a woman on a quest, hunting for a dress with pockets. I must have a way to bring the gloves into the house without carrying a purse. They need to be on my person and under my control.

The bell dings as I walk into the shop. A perky salesgirl welcomes me in. "Hi! Is there anything I can help you find today?" She asks.

"Oh, no thanks. I'm just browsing." I'm trying to stay unremarkable.

I go through the racks of dresses. My fingers run down the side of each dress until they hit paydirt. It's an adorable retro shift dress with bright colors and deep pockets. Perfect!

Okay! Murderous dress with pockets—check.

Now for the gloves: I drive to a pharmacy an hour away and pay with cash. Taking one pair out of the box, I throw the rest in the dumpster, along with the receipt. If my house or car is searched, there won't be anything to find.

I feel pretty good about my plan. I'm confident no one knows Jake is messing around with Chloe. That's good for me because it means no one would suspect I have any motive to want Jake dead. I can do this.

This murder is happening, and I might even get away with it.

CHAPTER TWENTY-SIX

Lizzy: Part Three
Night of the Murder

I've been waiting all evening for Jake to go to his office to do a little coke. It happens at every Carter party without fail. I've decided that will be my best chance. I'll stick the knife in his back while he's snorting all that money up his nose. I've got to be quick, though. In and out.

The hope is to kill him with the first strike. If I have to take it out for a second, the blood will be flung around the room and probably on me too. If that's the way it works out, I'm prepared to keep stabbing until he's dead. I will make sure he never touches Chloe again. I will kill him tonight, no matter what it takes.

After waiting all night for my chance, Jake finally heads for his office. *Oh no.* One of his soccer buddies is trailing behind him. This ruins my plan! My mind starts racing. *What am I supposed to do now?* I run through possible scenarios to get Jake alone. I can only think of one.

It isn't long before Jake returns from his office, rubbing his nose and sniffing hard. He and I are the only ones in the kitchen.

I take a quick peek around the room. Everyone is fully engaged in conversations. Nobody is even looking our way.

I sidle up to Jake and run my fingers up and down his muscular arm. "Jake," I purr, "I've lived next to you for ten years. You've tortured me long enough." I curl my fingers around his bicep. Leaning in, I whisper, "I have a husband who is out of town all the time. While you're right here." Jake turns to me with a lascivious smile. I go on. "I thought while no one is paying attention, we could run upstairs."

He is eager and grabs my hand, turning for the stairs. "Wait," I pull my hand, "No one can see us going up together. I'll go up the back stairs, and after a few minutes, you come up the front." I do my best come-hither smile.

"Okay, doll, see you there." He shoots me one more sneaky grin and goes into the living area. He's revolting.

I look over at the knives. The obvious choice is the one Kimber dried and replaced in the block earlier because I know it will be clean. Using that one feels like kismet. I take it as a sign that I'm doing the right thing. Jake is a pervert, a cheater, and a pedophile. Kimber and the kids will be better off without him.

Upstairs, I will have to play things by ear. This wasn't the plan, but I'm determined to go the distance. I make the decision to wait for Jake at the top of the stairs, this might actually work to my advantage if I play my cards right.

I'm a bundle of nerves, my mouth is dry, my legs are weak. It feels like I've been standing here forever. For a moment, I fear Jake won't come for me. But I didn't need to worry. Here he comes, rounding the corner and jogging up the stairs. My heart is pounding nearly out of my chest. *You can do this, Lizzy.*

You have to. It's now or never. As Jake reaches the last step, I pull the knife from behind my back and plunge it deep into his heart. I drive it in there with everything I have, just like he drove himself into my daughter. I feel the crunch as it passes his ribs and keep pushing until it won't go any farther.

I have no words for the look on Jake's face. He begins to fall backward. His mouth contorted, trying to say words that he will never get out. The knife's handle slides out of my hand as Jake falls. In slow motion, Jake's arms fly out to his sides. His hands grab at thin air, and then his back hits the stairs. He flips, then flips again, like a rag doll. I can hear his bones cracking.

When he comes to rest, I know he's dead. And, honestly, all I feel is relief. There is no pity in my heart for Jake Carter. He will never touch my Chloe again, and that's all that matters.

I peel the gloves off my hands and shove them deep into my pocket. It's time to get back to my island. On the way back, I see the door to the second-floor bathroom is closed. Someone is in there, and I don't want to be here when they open the door. I hustle back downstairs and retake my seat.

A glance around the room finds everyone as I left them. I try to calm myself down. *It's over, Lizzy. You did what you had to do.* Jake is dead.

I'm debating whether or not to open another bottle of wine when I hear feet trotting down the back stairs. It's Eli. At first, I assume it was him in the bathroom upstairs, but it is written all over his face. He saw me murder his brother. Eli *saw* it. There's not a doubt in my mind. He should be screaming at the top of his lungs that Jake is dead and I killed him, but he isn't.

I test the waters by asking him if he has tried the crab

croquettes. Eli answers me as if we are having a normal conversation. *He's not going to say anything.* I can't explain how I know, but something happens between us—a silent understanding. He will be my alibi.

Only a minute or two passes before we hear Kimber screaming. Eli and I exchange glances and run with everyone else toward the wailing.

Jake's broken body lies at Kimber's feet. Blood has started to spread on his shirt from his stab wound. A wound I'm responsible for. Jake is dead and I killed him.

You understand why I had to do it, don't you? That was my baby girl Jake was screwing. He would have broken her heart and ruined her life. I did what any mother would do.

You would do it too—right?

EPILOGUE

Kimber

One Year Later

It's such a beautiful day. Eli and Allie are in the pool, splashing around like teenagers, while young Liam plays in his little pen. I watch as he gnaws on a breadstick. He's the light in all our lives.

Cameron is doing cannonballs, upsetting Chloe and Josie as they float around with their noodles. I've been listening to the girls' conversation. It's all about Chloe's new boyfriend. She seems to be quite smitten. Much to Lizzy's relief, Chloe decided to stay local and attend Vanderbilt University. She lives on campus, but we see her all the time.

Lizzy is taking sun next to me, her eyes closed, a Kindle in her lap. She and I have been spending more and more time together. There are no more parties for me to obsess over, and John is still gone all the time. So, Lizzy and I fill the little gaps in each other's lives.

After Jake's death, I started going to therapy. I didn't understand all the things I was feeling. I actually grieved for him, missed him, and felt lost without him. Whatever bound us together was something I needed to understand and deal with. I'm still working on things, but I feel better every day.

Collin and Beth don't come over as much as they used to. Beth is afraid that I'll suddenly want to be with Collin. Of course, she has nothing to worry about, but I haven't pushed it. Collin and I will always love each other. We still 10-4 every day, but the physical distance is probably the healthiest thing for us all.

Jake's case is still open. They were never able to gather enough evidence to charge anyone. Detective Parker felt strongly that Greg Prescott was involved. But he never had enough to prove it. So life has gone on.

The kids are thriving. Life is good. I have no desire to ever be with a man again. I am at last fulfilled all by myself.

Who do I think killed Jake? Well, I know who it was. I saw Lizzy grab the knife from the block and head up the back stairs. A few minutes later, I saw Jake going into the foyer. Somehow, I knew. I could have stopped it, jumped up, and ran after my husband, warning him not to go upstairs. I could have, but I didn't.

When Lizzy returned to the kitchen without the knife, I was surprised to see Eli right behind her. I still don't know if he saw what happened between Lizzy and Jake or if he was somehow involved. It doesn't matter to me either way.

On that night, I didn't know what Lizzy's reasons were. It wasn't until the funeral that I put two and two together. Chloe cried for Jake as I should have. She wept as if she'd lost her greatest love. Right or wrong, her feelings were one hundred percent real to her. That being said, it doesn't make what Jake did any less disgusting. Chloe grew up with our own babies, and if I were Lizzy, I would have done the same thing.

I have never let on to anyone that I know. What purpose would it serve? It's best to let sleeping dogs lie. Jake is gone, and the world is a kinder place for it. My life has changed for the better.

I still like my wine in the evenings, but it isn't like it used to be. I don't feel like I *need* it. That's the difference. As for the stimulant, I haven't visited Killa since the day of the murder. I don't need him anymore, either.

You would think I would miss my parties, but I don't. The people here today are enough for me. And even better, I know I'm enough for them, exactly as I am.

FAITH FRANKLIN

FOOD FOR THOUGHT

Kimber's hand goes to her throat when she's afraid. This began after the first *episode*, when Jake strangled her. She even does it in front of the women at the island when Jake whispers *sweet nothings* into her ear. Yet, when Collin is bathing her, her head is thrown back and her throat exposed. She will always be safe with Collin.

Kimber tells Collin early on that she didn't plan on kissing anyone, and she never has. Jake only gives her kisses on the forehead. Kissing was too intimate for both of them.

Julian "Red" Herring. Well, the name speaks for itself. And it was no coincidence that his favorite drink was bourbon & *ginger*.

Julian's wife, Susan, is indeed pregnant. She has been nauseous for a week and only had one glass of wine at the party. Is Jake the father?

Your guess is as good as mine!

ABOUT THE AUTHOR

◆ ◆ ◆

Faith Franklin grew up on the west coast of Florida, spending sunny days playing in the Gulf of Mexico, her first love. She now resides in Louisville, KY with her husband and children, having traded her sea horses for thoroughbreds. Though, no matter where her feet are planted, her heart will always be floating in warm, salty waters.